DARK RIDE

IAIN ROB WRIGHT

 WANT FREE BOOKS?

Don't miss out on your FREE Iain Rob Wright horror starter pack. Five free bestselling horror novels sent straight to your inbox. No strings attached.

Visit the back of the book for more information.

FOREWORD

It's hard to believe that this will be my 26th novel. It's been a blessed 8 years that I still find difficult to accept as being my reality. As a kid I dreamed of being a writer like my heroes Stephen King, James Herbert, Terry Pratchett, RL Stine, and a hundred more, but it never felt like a possibility.

I was a troubled kid, living in a house with no carpets and cracked windows. My problems with anxiety started at an early age, and I would often try to escape my despair by indulging in fantasy. Books, films, and video games were a big part of my life, but so too was something else: wrestling.

I would get home from school on Friday nights and watch three hours of WCW followed by two hours of WWE. My mum would make me chicken sandwiches and I would have an entire bottle of Apple Tango next to me on my bed. It was the day of the week I looked forward to most. I loved spending time with my heroes and the villains in the ring. Giants like Goldberg, Hulk Hogan, Stone Cold, and the Rock. While I still take a slight interest in wrestling today, I have never loved it like I did in those days.

Today, my loves are different. I love my wife. I love my

children. And I love writing books for my readers. There is, however, a big kid still inside me, and a decade ago it discovered a new love — theme parks.

I was a poor kid, so Disney World was just some place rich kids went on about, and Universal Studios was just some place mentioned at the end of Clarissa Explains it All. As with most things I couldn't experience as a kid, I had convinced myself that theme parks and the like were rubbish. That's why, when I met my wife, Sally, and she suggested we do things like going to the theatre or on nice holidays, I would wrinkle my nose and decline. It was defensive programming to keep me from being envious or disappointed. It took a couple of years before Sally was able to start dragging me out of my shell.

The first time I allowed her to take me to the theatre, we went to see the Lion King at the Lyceum. The very first opening scene brought me to tears - Ooooeeeeeeesssvvveeeeennnnyaaaaaaa! I actually sobbed, and it was because I suddenly realised how wrong I had been. How stupid. The tough, council estate kid had crumbled and a man emerged that saw how wonderful the world could be. This thing happening on stage in front of me was amazing and emotional, but it had been there the whole time. Nothing had been keeping it from me except for my own cynicism and unwillingness to try new things. I had only needed to open up my mind.

Today, I go the theatre every chance I get. I love it, and it's remarkably affordable in most cases. Whether I am going to see a comedian, a show, a band, it turns into a fantastic evening every time and one that stays with me forever. I'll never forget seeing Donny Osmond in Chicago, or the entire cast of Nashville singing my favourite tunes. The theatre is like nothing else.

FOREWORD

Although I started to change as a person the night I saw the Lion King, I still had a ways to go. Sally wanted to go to Disney World, a place she had gone several times as a child. Again, I wrinkled my nose. Disney? Disney is for kids. I'm a tough guy and a grown man. I don't want to see Mickey bloody Mouse. Again, Sally wore me down eventually for my own good.

Being young and single, we were able to save a little and book a two week trip to Orlando on a shoe string. We didn't compromise on tickets though, and we got a full pass for all of the Disney Parks and all of the Universal ones. I didn't say so at the time, but I was starting to get excited. I had only ever been to Spain. Heading to America seemed unreal.

The moment we arrived at our cheap hotel (the Rodeway Inn) on International Drive, I was in love. The warm air, the clean grass, the amazing food... America was where I belonged. We bought Lynxx passes to get about, and within a couple of days I went from bewildered to at home. It was time to go to see Magic Kingdom.

The moment I set foot on the boat that would take us across lake Buena Vista, I gasped in awe. It was another milestone in the journey of who I am. Everything was so big, so beautiful, and people of all types were smiling. I didn't feel silly anymore for being a grown man at Disney, in fact I felt like an excited child. And I never let go of that child. I keep him with me in all that I do.

My first ride at Magic Kingdom was Stitch's Great Escape! I soon learned that it's pretty poor in comparison to everything else, but the theming and the experience was still like nothing I had ever witnessed before. I loved it, and after two weeks in Florida, I never wanted to go home. I wish I was there right now. My favourite place on Earth.

Today, I try to love as much of life as I can, but I would

never have opened up if Sally hadn't dragged me on a plane to Orlando. It showed me how vast and wonderful the world is if you work hard and commit to experiencing everything on offer. Rich or poor, there is always something new you can try, and you should. It's never too late to stop growing.

And so, theme parks and wrestling are a massive part of who I am today. One gave me hope as a child, and the other gave me hope as an adult. This horror novel would not have been possible without them and I hope it scares the pants off you like the Tower of Terror did me.

Love, as always,

Iain

We keep moving forward, opening new doors, and doing new things, because we're curious and curiosity keeps leading us down new paths.
— **Walt Disney**

I'm scared to death of rollercoaster rides.
— **Liam Neeson**

Sweet Cream on an ice cream sandwich!
— **The Rock**

Dedicated to my kids, for making every day a thrill ride.

CHAPTER ONE

"Oh my God, I think I'm going to throw up!"

Pamela rubbed her daughter's back, hoping it was an exaggeration. It usually was, but you never knew when the exception would be, when you would suddenly end up with puke all over you. "Take deep breaths, honey. Do you want to sit down?"

Eight-year-old Natalie shook her head, blonde pigtails flapping against her shoulders. "No, Mum. I want to go on again."

"Me too," said Nathan, tugging at his mother's sleeve.

Pamela glanced back over her shoulder. Then up at the *Thresher*. The rollercoaster had seemed okay at first, considering it didn't go upside down, but that first steep drop had sent her stomach into her mouth and it was yet to descend.

The twins had loved it though.

Could she really say no to them? They'd been through so much recently, and none of it their fault.

"Let Mummy have a rest and we'll go on again," she said, breathing in through her nose and out through her mouth. It was the same tactic she used when she saw or smelt something particularly stomach-churning on her ward. Even after fourteen years as a nurse, she still got nauseated by some of the things people came in with. Just last week, an elderly man came in so filthy with fungal infections that his entire groin had appeared ready to slough away in a miasma of blood and pus.

"Can't we ride it on our own?" Nathan asked in a whiny voice. His hair was getting long, delicate golden threads rising on the breeze. Pamela raised a hand to her own hair – mousy brown unlike her children's – and realised they were all overdue a cut. When had she become so unorganised?

She knew exactly when.

Cheating bastard.

"They won't let you on the ride without an adult, honey," Pamela told her son. "Let's go on something else, okay, and we'll come back later."

Both children pulled a face, but she didn't make a habit of lying to them. They trusted her word and allowed themselves to be led away, but she had to battle with them again when they passed a candyfloss stall. "Nope! Not until I see you eat some real food. Anyway, we're doing rides at the moment. What would you like to go on next?"

"I wanna go on the rapids," said Nathan.

Natalie nudged her brother and scowled. "We already got wet on the log flume. I want to go on the *Devil Spinner*."

Pamela's stomach sloshed at the mere name of it. With a groan, she asked, "Which one is that?"

Natalie pointed her tiny index finger, making the pink fairy ribbons tied around her wrist dance in the breeze. The ride she pointed to resembled a traditional fairground waltzer, but its spinning carts were mounted on a large whirling disc that travelled back and forth on a banana-shaped track. Rides were a lot more complicated nowadays, it seemed.

So that's two counts of spinning and one count of swinging back and forth. I thought the rollercoaster was bad.

"Can we do something with less spinning, please, angel? I don't think Mummy's stomach can handle any more right now."

Natalie pulled a face, but then brightened as she seemingly had another thought. Her sly smile was the same mischievous smirk she got whenever she snuck a chocolate bar out of the fridge without asking. Slowly and deliberately, she said, "I want to go on *Frenzy*."

"Okay, which one is *Frenzy*?"

"It's the new one," said Nathan, leaning against a pair of giant shields that made up part of the theming for one of the park's eateries – a large wooden cabin with a painted sign: the *Great Hunt*. "There'll be a massive queue for it."

A queue? Pamela sighed. *A queue means rest.*

She probed further. "What kind of ride is it? And stop leaning against that, please, Nathan. You'll get told off!"

Nathan moved away from the shields and folded his arms grumpily.

"It's like a ghost train," Natalie explained, seemingly knowing that the word *ghost* would count against her, so quickly glossing over it. "But it's not scary, Mum, I swear. Rebecca went on it the day it opened and said it's brilliant. Please, Mum, can we go on it? Dad would let us."

That stung Pamela, but she knew she shouldn't take it personally. She couldn't get upset every time the twins mentioned their father – or used him to blackmail her. They didn't know what a bastard he was, and while she would love to tell them, she never would. Couldn't.

Pamela thought she knew all the rides at *Saxon Hills* – the place had been running since she was a kid herself – but she hadn't heard of this one. It didn't sound age-appropriate, but the twins had been forced to grow up fast with the divorce. Should she give them some leeway?

"Point the ride out to me," she said, "and I'll have a look. If the line isn't too long, and if it doesn't look too scary, we can go on, okay?"

Natalie hopped and cheered. Nathan rolled his eyes, but smiled too. He'd probably only objected initially out of a habit of arguing with his sister. They argued more and more lately, but they both loved rides. Had loved them ever since going on a junior carousel at the fair. They had been just two years old. Pamela still remembered the day well. They had all been together. A family unit of four instead of a fractured three in two separate configurations.

Natalie took off, leading them through the park. Pamela wondered how she'd missed all the posters featuring this new *Frenzy* ride. As the latest amusement ride, it was seemingly advertised all over the park. One poster, pasted against the side of *King Alfred's Hog Roast*, stated in sinister lettering: *Woden's Frenzy: Escape the fury of the elder god.*

It didn't sound suitable for eight-year-olds, but...

She should at least check it out. They would only complain to their father if she was too strict, and he, of course, would take their side – be their buddy. Any more of her soon-to-be ex-husband playing the 'good guy' and she might lose her mind. It was easy being the fun parent when you only saw the kids twice a week, but she, of course, had to take care of the homework, hygiene, and hollering. Anything that put a frown on the twin's faces was her responsibility, while junk food and video games were their father's remit. And didn't he just love it.

Pamela felt she was losing her children right in front of

her, powerless to prevent it. The reason it hurt so much was because she had done nothing wrong.

Except love their father.

Come on! Just enjoy today, Pam. The twins are happy. They are happy with you. He's not here, so don't let him ruin this. You're having fun.

Wow, that's right. I'm actually having fun. I thought I'd lost the ability.

The three of them jogged across a set of narrow steel tracks belonging to the park's miniature steam train, then they crossed a bridge over the river rapids. Nathan leapt up and tried to direct a water cannon at one of the passing dinghies, but it was broken. Something he seemed reluctant to accept.

"Just leave it, Nathan," his sister chided. "You're wasting ride time."

Glumly, Nathan peeled himself away from the cannon and hurried to catch them up.

And then they saw it.

Pamela was impressed. But not in a good way.

Frenzy's entrance was housed inside a massive bronze helmet with wings sprouting from either side. The giant prop was the height of a double-decker bus, and buried in its recesses were two glowing red eyes that seemed to hover in darkness. Now and then the helmet filled with steam, making anyone caught in the blast squeal. Powerful speakers boomed out mocking laughter.

The ride's signage was made from tree branches and vines, twisted around rocks. F-R-E-N-Z-Y.

"This is so cool," said Nathan, walking forward with his mouth hanging open. Natalie was equally enthralled, unable to say anything at all. She stared with wide, hungry eyes at the giant staring helmet. A queue of excited people formed beneath it.

Everything Pamela was seeing told her to turn around and find a ride more suitable – maybe even go on the *Thresher* again – but the needful expressions of her children tugged at her emotions like fish hooks in her skin. She was tired of always being the one to say no. She was tired of being the bad guy.

"I-It looks a bit scary, guys. I don't want you both getting nightmares."

Nathan pulled a face. "It's just a ride, Mum. It's not real."

"Yeah," Natalie agreed. "We won't get scared, I promise. And *you'll* be with us."

Pamela sighed. If she was honest, the only person who had screamed with any amount of fear today had been her. The twins were having the time of their lives. Should she just let them get on with it?

If the height restriction allows them in, it must be okay, right?

"Okay," she said after a moment's thought. "If you're allowed to go on it then… okay."

Both her children rushed her, making her instinctively cover up. They collided with her without fear and threw their arms around her waist in a massive embrace. She found herself beaming uncontrollably.

"Thanks, Mum."

"Love you, Mum."

"I love you too. Come on, we still have to queue."

They headed towards that giant leering helmet. To join the queue, they would have to pass beneath it.

Towards that mocking laughter.

Here goes nothing. Oh balls!

The screams didn't translate at first. They were in a theme park after all, the one place where screams were ordinary. It wasn't until they joined the tail end of the queue that she realised the screams were different. They were not notes tinged with glee and amusement.

They were the screams of people screaming in terror.

It was difficult to see the front of the queue, but it appeared to end at a square building covered in vines and leaves – like a troll's cave. The screams seemed to be coming from there.

Suddenly anxious, Pamela grabbed her twins by the slack of their T-shirts, fists full of cotton. Both children complained, not yet realising that something was wrong, and wondering why they were being stopped when the queue was right in front of them.

"Please don't change your mind," Natalie begged.

"I haven't, just hold on a sec." Pamela stood stock still, keeping her children next to her. She focused on what she was hearing.

Then on what she was smelling.

Smoke. Oh my God, something's burning.

"I can smell fire," said Nathan, scrunching up his nose like a bloodhound.

The screams turned from terror to agony as a bloom of dirty black smoke billowed from beyond the huddled mass of queuing people. The ride, hidden beyond the themed entrance, was on fire. *Frenzy* was burning.

My kids could have been on it! Five minutes earlier and we would have been on it.

A member of staff, wearing a red baseball cap and a red polo shirt, snaked his way through the queue, barging people aside as he sought to make it out of the helmet. It looked like he was going for help.

Please let it arrive soon.

People further along the queue, near the ride building,

started moving away. A mother screamed that her son and husband were on the ride, but other people held her back.

Then things got worse.

A figure stumbled out of the ride building and into the shocked crowd. The young man was smouldering, clothes blackened and seared into the bubbling pink flesh of his arms and shoulders. Only a few stray patches of hair remained on his glistening red scalp.

The man fell to his knees and waved a smoking arm, pointing back towards the ride's building. "T-Trapped," he said in a strangled voice. "Th-They're all trapped!"

The man fell forward, exposing the slick, exposed flesh of his back. It looked like raw chicken.

Pamela dragged her children away before they were traumatised forever, then huddled anxiously with them as a stampede erupted.

Natalie looked at her. "Mummy, what's happening?"

"I don't know, sweetheart. I don't know."

"It's something bad," said Nathan, and she couldn't speak to argue with him.

Something exploded, making the fleeing crowd scream. A massive ball of fire rose from behind the giant bronze helmet and lit up the grey sky.

Those glowing red eyes stared at Pamela. The mocking laughter continued pumping from the speakers. It even seemed to get louder, faster.

More frenzied.

"Look away, kids. Please, just look away."

CHAPTER TWO

Twelve years later...

AJ RAISED his forearm and wiped blood from his eyes. People yelled abuse from every direction. A small boy spat at him.

It was glorious.

The *Human Tractor* threw a running clothesline but AJ ducked and hit the ropes, then rebounded and delivered a solid drop kick. Tractor, a twenty-stone *big man,* dragged himself over to the turnbuckle for a rest.

AJ went back to tearing apart a *Leeds United* football shirt in the centre of the ring – an act utterly infuriating to the three hundred Leeds residents in attendance tonight. It was cheap heat, but it was good heat.

He was on fire.

AJ threw the torn football shirt down on the canvass and stomped on it. He marched over to Tractor and gave the big man a kick as he lay there with his huge gut on display. He needed a time-out to catch his breath, because, aside from being fat, the guy was pushing fifty.

AJ stooped and adjusted one of his bright pink tasselled kneepads. It was almost time for the main spot of the match, so he went over to the ropes and gloated at the crowd. They booed and hissed from behind the barricade as he flexed his biceps and kissed each impressive bulge.

Wait for it!

"Don't hate me because I'm better than you," he yelled at the crowd. "Hey, baby, I see you looking at me. You want a piece of this?"

Any second now. Come on!

AJ climbed up on the bottom rope and leant over the top one, continuing to taunt the crowd. "Hey you, did you dress yourself this morning or did Mummy do it?"

The canvass bounced behind AJ as lumbering footsteps gathered speed.

Here it comes. Right on schedule.

He gripped the top rope tightly. Took in a breath and held it. A forearm struck him between the shoulder blades and he went toppling forward. Using his left hand and abdomen as a fulcrum, he tumbled over the top rope and crashed to the arena floor eight feet below. He hit the mats perfectly with both feet flat on the floor.

A perfect spot.

The crowd roared with delight at the gloating heel being knocked on his ass mid-taunt. AJ had them in the palm of his hand. Like he did every night.

But tonight was different.

Tonight, there was a road agent in the audience. Terry Spakes from the big leagues. America. This was AJ's chance to show what he could do.

This was his moment.

Pretending to have had the stuffing knocked out of him, AJ clambered to his feet. He then took a risk and flopped forward against the crowd railing, allowing the baleful fans to get their hands on him. They slapped and shoved at him gleefully, but none too hard. Most fans understood the game.

The next spot was about to happen.

AJ pushed himself away from the railing, keeping his back to the ring. He shook his head as if shaking off cobwebs and resumed shouting insults at the crowd. How dare they enjoy his pain? How dare they laugh at him? He was the greatest of all time, didn't they know? They weren't fit to lick his boots. He was *Bright Lights*, baby!

His vision suddenly went blurry. A little blood still leaked from his right eyebrow, a split caused by Tractor's errant fist, so he wiped at it with his bright pink wristband. His vision remained blurry.

He wiped again.

Still blurry.

What the hell?

AJ heard the canvass vibrate. No time left. He should already be turning around.

But I can't see!

Knowing Blue Stormer was about to leap over the top rope and come down right on top of him, AJ turned quickly. He needed to plant his feet and catch his opponent, but by the time he was facing the ring, Stormer was already airborne. The lad was tiny by wrestling standards – only five foot nine – but *holy shit* could he fly. He cleared the top rope by half a foot and sailed out of the ring with his arms outstretched like an eagle.

Cameras clicked. LEDs flashed.

The crowd gasped.

AJ opened up his body, trying to make himself into a human crash mat.

More LEDs flashed.

AJ's vision swirled.

Time slowed.

Stormer came down hard, his chest clonking against AJ's shoulder and bouncing off. AJ tried to grab him with both arms but caught nothing but air. Both men hit the mats hard.

AJ lay on his back. He took two breaths and waited for something to hurt. When nothing did, he rolled over onto his side and surveyed the damaged. His vision was still blurry, but it was beginning to clear, so he could make out Stormer lying on his back nearby. He was staring up at the lights and panting. AJ was close enough to reach out and touch him, but that would break the illusion that they were bitter enemies. *Kayfabe* was the word the industry used, and it meant you kept up the illusion that everything was real no matter what. The curtain must always stay down. Heels like AJ didn't show concern for their opponents. He still needed to know that Stormer was okay though. "Dillon? You okay, brother?"

The referee, Graham, was already checking on Dillon, obviously concerned by his hard landing. To facilitate the conversation, Graham leant over Dillon and shielded him, so that the crowd couldn't see them talking. Dillon turned his masked face, only his eyes and mouth visible, then muttered, "I'm hurt, brother. We need to go home."

AJ groaned. 'Going home' was code for ending the match, but they were supposed to go another five minutes. The planned ending included Graham taking a 'ref bump', allowing AJ to hit Tractor with an illegal chair shot. He would then pin the fat bastard and steal the win. That wasn't going to work now though. The match would end sloppy.

No helping it. Dillon's hurt. And it's all my fault. I missed the catch.

I never miss the catch...

AJ climbed to his feet, his shoulder bothering him. Gently, he clutched the back of Dillon's mask and pulled the guy up. Dillon slumped against the apron but allowed himself to be rolled back inside the ring. The lad was too much of a professional not to finish the match without a pin.

Tractor was back on his feet and ready to deliver a beat down. He was unaware of the situation, so Graham, doing his true job as a referee – directing the match and its timings – had to hurry over and whisper an update. Tractor swore when he heard the news, and as soon as AJ rolled underneath the bottom rope, he got clobbered. "Here's your receipt, bitch." Tractor thumped him again, striking his shoulder and causing him to yell.

"Cool it, man. We need to go home."

Tractor grabbed AJ by his long, wavy blonde hair and got him in a side headlock. "The finish is you and me. Dillon only has to stay down."

"He's hurt!"

"So will you be if you botch our ending. Terry Spakes is watching from Gorilla. I ain't screwing up tonight, boy."

AJ went to argue, but Tractor clubbed him in the back and legitimately knocked the wind out of him. The bastard was giving him a receipt for hurting Dillon, but that wasn't his right.

AJ crawled towards the ropes, not having to act hurt because his shoulder was genuinely throbbing. He clambered to his feet and Tractor came for him, but this time AJ retaliated by throwing an elbow into the big man's gut. Knowing that Terry Spakes was watching from the Gorilla Position – the area just behind the curtains through which the wrestlers made their entrance – Tractor had no choice but to sell the blow like a professional. He clutched his gut and let out a loud *ooph!*

AJ struck again with backhanded chops, making Tractor stagger backwards on his heels. After the third and hardest chop, Tractor was off balance, so AJ leapt in the air and delivered his patented A-Kick. It was only a spinning back kick, but as one of his signature moves, Tractor was duty-bound to sell it and hit the mat. You didn't no-sell another guy's signature moves.

Now in the ring with two downed opponents, AJ moved over to the referee. "Graham, Tractor's gone into business for himself. I'm going to pin Dillon and go home, okay?"

To his surprise, Graham shook his head. "Tractor says we do the ending as planned. Sorry, AJ."

AJ clutched his gut like he was trying to catch his breath, but all he was really doing was disguising their conversation. He couldn't let the crowd see him in the ring having a chitchat. "Sod that. Dillon's hurt."

"He's not involved in the ending. Toss him to the floor and the guys will check on him."

AJ knew Dillon pretty well – a tough kid from Yorkshire. If he wanted to abort the planned finish, it was because he was legitimately hurt, not because he was being a pussy. Tractor, on the other hand, was a piece-of-shit bully. A tub of lard with no moves and no sell. But he was also one of the show's bookers. Tractor had been in the game more than twenty years, and part of the seed money for tonight's show had come straight out of his pocket. Graham was right – Tractor was the boss here.

AJ snarled. "Fine! Tractor wants a finish, I'll sodding give him one."

Dillon was lying still at the edge of the ring and clutching his wrist. AJ dropped and got him in a rear chokehold, cradling him gently even though it appeared violent and painful. He put his mouth next to Dillon's ear and whispered. "Hey, brother. I'm sorry, but Tractor won't let us go home. I'm gonna throw you out and then you're done."

"I think my wrist's broken, AJ."

AJ clenched his jaw, wanting to apologise over and over, but knowing he couldn't do it right at this moment. "I'll make things right, brother, I promise."

He thrust Dillon backwards, pretending to strike the wrestler's skull against the canvass, then kicked him out of the ring like a bag of rubbish. A pair of first aiders immediately ran to help him on the arena floor. That was something at least.

How did I screw up so badly? I've hit that spot a hundred times. My timing was all wrong. My positioning...

Because I couldn't bloody well see properly.

A blow to AJ's shoulder knocked him from his thinking. Pain bolted up his neck and made him wince. Tractor had struck him in the shoulder twice now, making it clear that the prick was targeting his injury.

Okay, that does it.

AJ went through the motions, taking Tractor's clumsy onslaught through gritted teeth. As a traditional 'big man', Tractor was all chops and punches, with his only other move being a big splash to put people away. Like AJ, he was a 'heel' – a bad guy – which meant the crowd began to cool as the two of them fought. They wanted to see Blue Stormer face off against the villains as the outnumbered underdog. Now it looked like Tractor and AJ would simply knock lumps out of one another instead.

Might as well make it count for something.

AJ dodged a punch from Tractor by ducking and spinning. He then unleashed a hellish backhanded slap across the big man's flabby chest – the hardest chop he had ever delivered. The crack echoed off the rafters.

The crowd groaned.

Tractor doubled over, holding a forearm across his chest. But AJ wasn't done. He grabbed Tractor by his long, greasy hair and forced him back up. He then unleashed another chop, even harder than the one before.

Tractor doubled over again, this time cursing out loud. He tried to resist AJ grappling him, but AJ wasn't playing around. He shoved the big man back against the turnbuckle and chopped his chest for a third time. Tractor's flabby pecs were bright red with angry-looking welts. AJ slapped him two more times, drawing thin beads of blood.

"Enough!" Tractor hissed. "Do it again and I'll fucking kill you."

"Not if I kill you first." AJ chopped Tractor a further two times, then, before the big man could recover, he mounted the middle turnbuckle and trapped him between his legs. Raising a fist in the air, AJ nodded to the crowd. Was this what they wanted to see?

The crowd cheered and whistled. Despite being a heel, they were on AJ's side now – easily flipped in the drama of the moment. They hated Tractor more than they hated him, and not just because the big man was a heel. They hated him because they knew he was a bully with a limited move-set and no charisma, while AJ and Dillon were two guys willing to break their bodies – literally – to entertain the crowd. Yes, they very much wanted to see this.

AJ, AJ, AJ...

AJ delivered the first punch, pulling the blow slightly but not all the way. He felt his knuckles knock against Tractor's skull, but it was nothing more than a love-tap really, cushioned even more by the pink wraps around his hands. As much as he would like to kick the shit out of Tractor, you couldn't take liberties with someone trusting you to keep them safe in the ring. The chops to the chest had been enough to make a point. Anything more serious would have to wait for the locker room.

The crowd roared. "One!"

AJ thumped Tractor again.

"Two!"

Again.

"Three!"

AJ took them up to nine, before pausing and letting them anticipate the final blow.

"TEEEEEEEEEE—

AJ punched Tractor on the head again.

—EN!"

AJ then hopped backwards off the turnbuckle, freeing Tractor from between his thighs. The big man hit one of his character spots, marching forward two steps as though he was perfectly fine, before flopping suddenly onto his face. Rick Flair did the spot better, but it wasn't a bad effort.

Graham placed a hand on AJ's bicep and pulled him back a step. "Easy, Alex, you're not supposed to be getting pops."

"We can't go heel on heel. We're losing the crowd."

Graham shook his head and sighed. "There's going to be hell to pay for this. It's a right shit-show."

AJ nodded to the roaring crowd. "I got the fans back. You hear them? I'll deal with the blowback afterwards, but let's give the kids what they came for."

Graham nodded. The two of them had known each other a long time, and as much as the old guy loved having a job, he loved the business more. And this was business.

AJ stood over Tractor, who was now slumped on his side. "We good, brother?"

"No," came the muffled reply. "You're a dead man."

"Let's do the spot and go home, okay? I'm gonna work

the crowd, you pull me down on top of Graham. We'll do the ending as best we can by ourselves."

Tractor didn't reply.

AJ gave him a toe-tap to the ribs. "You with me or not?"

Tractor hissed. "I'm with you."

As much as Tractor was a bully who took liberties in the ring, he was also a veteran. He wouldn't screw with the plan once agreed.

AJ headed to the turnbuckle and climbed up onto the middle rope. He threw his hands up in a classic 'face' pose and the crowd popped for him again. All memories of having hated him five minutes ago disappeared. He was 'Bright Lights' AJ Star. The hottest wrestler in the universe.

"What's the plan?" Graham stood to his left, looking up at him and pretending to tell him off. Climbing the turnbuckle was technically illegal in a wrestling match.

AJ spoke out the corner of his mouth. "Just stay where you are and get ready to bump."

"Roger that."

AJ felt the canvass bounce and knew Tractor was getting to his feet. He continued working the crowd, acting oblivious as they shouted warnings at him. *Behind you! Watch out! AJ, look!*

Dillon lay next to the crowd barricade on the floor. The first aiders could do nothing but console him. AJ's stomach churned. He'd delivered the odd black eye in his time between the ropes, but he'd never seriously hurt anyone.

Until now.

Tractor grabbed AJ by the back of his bright pink tights and yanked him backwards. It was sloppy, and AJ had to fall unconvincingly to his left. He collapsed on top of Graham, and the referee flew backwards as if a train had hit him, immediately feigning unconsciousness on the canvass. A classic ref bump.

AJ pretended to be hurt and rolled out of the ring. Tractor lumbered out after him, so AJ turned and punched the guy. He kept things slow so that Tractor could block him, and the big man raised a forearm like a shield before delivering a thumping head butt that sent AJ reeling. That was part of the agreed upon spot.

AJ wheeled around and fell to his knees, then flopped against an empty seat the ring announcer had vacated when she'd seen the two of them coming. The aluminium seat was foldable, and AJ quickly closed it flat. This happened out of Tractor's sight as the big man stood directly behind him. That was why he didn't see it coming when AJ leapt up and brought the folded chair down on his head.

It was a rare spot nowadays, to see a chair shot right to the skull, but Tractor had been adamant before the match about doing things old-school. To give the guy credit, he had a noggin like a bowling ball.

Tractor sprawled back against the ring apron while AJ raised the chair above his head a second time. He delayed for a moment to work up the crowd then brought it down again.

Tractor threw himself under the ropes and back inside the ring. He made it up onto his knees but then crumpled into a ball. This he did purposefully so that he could 'blade' himself. Unlike AJ, who had been opened up the 'hard way' earlier by a clumsy punch, Tractor would produce a concealed razor blade from his wrist tapes and use it to slice along the upper edge of his eyebrow, producing a lot of blood from a pretty insubstantial wound. It was a trick of the trade, a century old.

AJ's own wound had finally stopped bleeding, which was

why it caused him to hesitate when his vision once again blurred. He rubbed at his eyes but there was no blood to clear. Two seconds passed and his vision returned to normal, but the brief disorientation had, once again, knocked him off his game.

Jesus, let's just get this over with.

AJ rolled into the ring, taking the 'steel' chair with him. Tractor rose up on his knees, revealing his blood-soaked face to the crowd – a 'crimson mask' – and the crowd roared with excitement. AJ lifted the chair again and pushed them over the edge. This time, instead of whacking the chair off the big man's head, he tossed it so that Tractor caught it. Then he jumped into the air and delivered an A-Kick that connected with the chair and drove it into Tractor's face.

Crack!

Tractor wobbled on his knees, blood dripping down his naked chest, then, like an uprooted oak tree, he toppled over and hit the canvass.

Timbeeerrr!

AJ made the pin just as Graham woke up and was miraculously able to make the count.

One...

Two...

Three!

The bell rang.

The crowd went wild.

CHAPTER THREE

Two weeks later...

AJ KNEW he shouldn't have been doing sixty in a forty, but a mixture of being late and being excited prevented him from lifting his foot off the accelerator. He'd arranged this trip, and at this rate he'd be the last one to arrive – something that filled him with an unreasonable amount of dread. It took him back to his days of heading off to primary school each morning with his mum. Always the last kid walking through the gates, long after the bell had rung.

AJ had arranged to meet the others at the train station in town, which was why he eventually found himself stuck behind a pair of spluttering city buses. He wasn't usually an impatient driver, but this afternoon he banged his fists against the steering wheel and yelled, "Come on, come on!"

They wouldn't mind him being late, he knew, but it had taken him the best part of a year to persuade them to come on this weekend, and it had to be the best time ever.

I don't want to waste a single minute.

After attempting to overtake the two ridiculously slow buses several times and failing, he was forced to wait until he reached the end of the road. He turned right while both buses mercifully turned left. The train station was on the next road.

His friends were waiting for him outside the ticket office, clutching cups of coffee and tea in polystyrene cups. Samantha was the first to recognise his beat-up Land Rover, so it was she who waved a hand first as he pulled up and parked. Samantha was his oldest friend. He hadn't seen her in months.

AJ hopped out from behind the wheel and slammed the driver-side door. He joined everybody at the ticket office. "Hey, the gang's all here!"

Samantha gave him a hug right away, and so did his other high school friend, Ashley. Her boyfriend, Greg, gave a manly handshake, while Ben, in his wheelchair, gave a cool nod. Ben's sister Tasha stood behind him and waved.

"Thought you were going to cancel on us," said Greg. His vest today was two sizes too small, but he had the body to pull it off. He dressed just like you would expect a personal trainer to dress. Even his shaved head had muscles.

"Sorry, everyone," said AJ. "I slept badly. Hurt my shoulder in a match a couple of weeks ago and it throbs like hell during the night. The doc wanted to give me painkillers, but it's a slippery slope in my game."

Greg folded his thick arms and looked concerned. "I'll take a look at it for you later, buddy. Sounds like you might have torn something. You should have seen me right after it happened."

AJ rolled his shoulder, displaying that it wasn't as bad as all that. "I've had plenty worse. Don't worry about it."

"So we gonna do this thing?" asked Ben. He was the third of AJ's school friends, and back in the day, along with Samantha and Ashley, they'd made an inseparable gang of four. "I'm ready to crack open the beers," he said. "Been on my feet all day."

AJ winced. "You going to be making wheelchair jokes all weekend?"

"It's part of my stand-up routine."

Everyone groaned.

"I'll go start loading up the booze," said Tasha. She was younger than the rest of them by several years – a fact made clear by her funky pink-and-black dreads – but she fitted in well enough. "Someone want to lend me a hand?"

"Yeah, I got you, T." Greg went with her over to the seven-seater Grand Picasso she used as part of her job at the care home. Both sides were covered in fading boldface lettering: **Crystal Glades Nursing Home**.

"So how you been?" Samantha asked AJ as they waited. Her blonde hair was in a ponytail today, as it usually was, but it seemed shorter than the last time he'd seen her. Back in school, people had sometimes mistaken them as brother and sister, with their matching yellow locks, but now his hair was longer than hers, and she had turned a little more towards brunette. "I haven't seen you in ages, AJ."

"I know, I know," he said. "I've been touring up and down the country non-stop. This weekend is the first break I've had in ages. I've been looking forward to it for months."

"Me too. How's your mum?"

"Oh, um, yeah, she's good. You'll have to drop by sometime. We'll have lunch. She misses you."

"Yeah, that'll be nice. I'll check my diary."

AJ knew her diary would be full. It always was lately. He took his share of the blame for being too busy as well, but the last several times they'd arranged to meet, it had been *she* who had cancelled.

We used to see each other so often. What happened?

After high school had ended, he and Samantha both went into jobs with the same tile company. AJ had been a part-time wrestler during most of that time, but two years ago he had started making enough money to do it as a full-time gig. Samantha, at the same time, had left the tile company to start her own accountancy business. She'd been busy every day since. He understood that, but he missed how close they had been.

AJ didn't want to dwell on regret, so he turned to Ashley. She looked stick-thin in her skinny jeans and vest top, and it made her wild red hair seem even more enormous. "How are things with you, Ash? Got many photography gigs on the cards?"

"Loads, thanks. It's really taken off lately. I'm having to turn people away. Weddings and christenings mostly, although I've started doing corporate work too. Not that exciting, but it pays the bills. Greg and I hardly see each other lately because of how busy we both are."

"That sucks, but I'm glad you're doing well. You remembered your camera for this weekend, right?"

She patted the leather satchel on her bony hip. "Never go anywhere without it."

AJ grinned. Ashley intended to take photographs for her portfolio, but she would also be taking pictures of them all having fun. Mementos of a weekend he wanted them to remember.

That I want to remember.

Ben turned his wheelchair. "Heads up. Beer's here."

Greg stomped across the car park with two large crates of lager under his thick arms. Tasha walked beside him with three carrier bags full of wine. They were all going to get bladdered this weekend, no doubt about it. AJ had already loaded a couple of crates in the back himself.

"Let's put it in my car." AJ headed to his Land Rover and opened the rear door. There wasn't a lot of space left, with the booze, camping supplies, and pop-up seat he'd raised for one of them to sit in, but they would cram in somehow.

"Crack one open," said Ben eagerly.

Greg placed the beer crates in the Land Rover and frowned. "What, *now*? We're about to get in the car."

"What's your point? I ain't driving. Beer me up."

"Me too," said Ashley. "I want to let my hair down."

Greg frowned at her. "Your hair is always down. It refuses to be restrained."

Ashley flipped her thick red frizz over her shoulder. "Just a reflection of my free spirit."

AJ chuckled. What was the harm in starting early? They were there to have fun, after all. "I can have one beer and still drive legally. Let's make a toast. To friendship."

"And to bright futures," Ben added.

Greg dug out beers for everyone, and they drank them in the car park like a bunch of students. AJ didn't want to toast to the future. He only wanted to enjoy this moment and the ones to follow. His smile was troubled as Ashley took his picture. He hoped the ones she took later would be better.

CHAPTER FOUR

"You really need to clean your car," said Ashley from the small pop-up seat in the Land Rover's rear. "It's really gross back here. I found a sock."

"Yeah, sorry about that," said AJ, taking his eyes from the road for a moment to look back at her. "Things have been a bit hectic lately."

"You think a sock is bad," said Tasha. "I sat on a toothbrush."

AJ grimaced. "Sorry! Life on the road."

Ben started to sing. "Free love on the free love freeway... Let's get some tunes on in here."

Samantha sat in the front passenger seat, fiddling with the radio. "You need to get a car with Bluetooth, you know that? Don't all cars have it nowadays?"

He side-eyed her. "You were with me when I bought this thing. If you had a problem with it, you should've said so at the time."

"I didn't have a problem with it *then*. Four years ago. We both still worked at Alscon when you got this tank, and it was *already* ancient."

He chuckled. "Hey, did you hear Alscon went bust? Some dodgy business went down and John did a runner. Disappeared off the face of the earth along with a handful of staff."

Samantha tutted. "Doesn't surprise me. That place always was a den of crooks. Part of the reason I left."

"Yeah, me too. I couldn't stand working with that Monty a moment longer. I swear the dickhead used to steal my leads."

"I thought you left because wrestling was your dream," said Greg from the seat behind him. "You told me you were going to be the next Simon Michaels."

AJ looked in the rear-view mirror at his friend and groaned. "*Shawn* Michaels. And I'm still working on it."

"Better get a move on," said Ben, wedged between the car seat and the folded up wheelchair crammed against his knees. "The big 3-0 is just around the corner."

"Hey, I don't turn thirty for another three months. I have plenty of time to make it."

"You already *have* made it," Samantha told him, patting his knee. "I read an article online saying you were one of the most respected wrestlers in the UK. What was it the writer said... oh yeah, that's it – he said you were the 'total package. Deceptively agile, remarkably strong, and delightfully charismatic'."

AJ felt himself blush. "Yeah, I read that article too. It was from the *Ringside Observer*. I got the number four spot in their power rankings."

"You see?" Samantha glared back at the others. "AJ is a wresting legend in the making. We should all be bowing at his feet."

Greg huffed. "Yeah, if wrestling was a real sport."

AJ snorted. "Your mother thought I was real enough when I was f—"

"Hey!" said Ben. "Let's leave mums out of it, okay? No need to go there. I won't stand for it."

Everyone laughed. They had known each other long enough to take every insult with a pinch of salt. AJ knew his friends were proud of him, as he was proud of them. They had all grown up a lot during the last few years, and the drunken nights of their mid-twenties were a long time past. Not that they couldn't be revisited from time to time.

"So what's the name of this place we're going to again?" Samantha retightened the band around her ponytail and tucked the few remaining gold strands behind her ears. "Sorry, I forgot."

AJ spoke loudly, making sure they could all hear. "We're going to *Saxon Hills*. One of the UK's oldest theme parks until its closure in 2009."

Ashley leant forward over the middle seats. "Why did it close?"

AJ shrugged. "Lot of reasons. Falling ticket sales, ageing rides, competition from Alton Towers and Drayton Manor. What really sealed Saxon Hills' fate, though, was the deadly accident that occurred in the summer of 2007."

"Here we go," said Samantha with a sly grin. "Our tour guide has arrived."

AJ chuckled and put on a mock authoritative tone. "At the turn of the century, Saxon Hills' owners invested heavily in the development of a new dark ride called *Frenzy*. Nothing like it had existed in the United Kingdom at the time, and its completion in 2006 led to a brief resurgence for the park. It was the owner's last roll of the dice to turn business around, and it seemed to have paid off."

"But it exploded," said Ben. "Or did they build it out of asbestos? Don't tell me, Womble infestation?"

AJ tutted. "No, nothing like that. A lunatic set Frenzy on

fire while fourteen people were trapped inside. Because of the narrow walkways, and there being only one fire escape, a mere five of those fourteen people escaped the fire, although one died immediately afterwards. Those trapped inside all burned to death, including Donal McCann, the madman who started the fire. He thought the ride was blasphemous."

"Blasphemous?" said Ashley.

"Yeah. Donal was a groundsman at the park, and for weeks he had been complaining to his colleagues about the ride being evil. What no one realised was that he had been stockpiling petrol inside the ride, intending to torch the place to the ground. He finally decided to go through with it one day while the ride was full of passengers. The youngest victim was a nine-year-old boy named Billy Scott. He'd been riding with his dad."

Samantha groaned and covered her mouth. "That's horrible. I'm glad the park shut down."

"You have to remember," said AJ, "that the fire was lit intentionally. It wasn't the park operator's fault."

"No," said Greg, "but the fact that no one could get out after the fire started was."

AJ nodded. "Which is what a court found. Saxon Hills' owners had to pay out millions to the families of the dead and injured. Frenzy was rapidly rebuilt and relaunched, the owners hoping to rescue some of the monumental cost they had already sunk into it, but people were reluctant to ride it after what had happened. The owners filed for bankruptcy and the park changed hands twice in the years that followed. Then, in 2009, Saxon Hills closed forever. Today is the ten-year anniversary of the last day the park accepted guests."

Ashley started gathering her frizzy red hair into bunches. It was an anxiety behaviour she'd displayed since the day they'd met as kids. "And it's totally abandoned now?" she said. "I still don't get why we're going there."

AJ smiled. "Derbyshire County Council reacquired the land, but they did nothing with it. Some rides were dismantled and sold off, but great chunks of the park were left sitting there to rust. It's a theme park graveyard. The perfect place to party."

"Place better not be haunted," said Tasha. "The ghost of Donal McCann could be stalking the place right now, for all we know."

Ben rolled his eyes. "Sis, you gotta stop watching TV so late at night. No such thing as ghosts."

"Spirits are all around us, whether or not you believe in them. And the spirits of those poor dead people might still be at the park, stuck forever in limbo. First sign of any freaky shit and I'm getting a taxi home. Don't know why you lot want to do this, anyway. It's well weird."

"You could always get your own friends," said Ben.

"I suppose it could be pretty cool," said Ashley, blowing an unruly strand of hair out of her face. "We could be the first people to visit this place in years. It's like we're explorers."

"Yeah," said AJ, "that's exactly how I feel."

"Hey," said Ben. "When white people go exploring, they have a habit of coming back with a bunch of brothers chained up in loincloths. This isn't an expedition, people, let's get that straight."

Ashley giggled nervously. "That doesn't happen any more though, right? Does it? It doesn't. No. Ha!"

"All the same," said Tasha with a smirk, "we'll be watching you white folk carefully."

More laughter. There was nothing Ben and Tasha wouldn't joke about, and that was a good quality in AJ's opinion. Serious people were the worst. If you couldn't have fun, the least you could do was fake it.

"How long's the drive?" Greg asked him.

"I'm about to pull onto the motorway. Journey'll take about an hour 'n' a half, I reckon."

"That's fine," said Ben, adjusting his wheelchair to give his knees another inch of room. "Gives us time to chill. Ashley, can you reach those beers in the back?"

"Um, yeah, I think so."

"Then crack 'em open, baby. The party starts now!"

Samantha turned back to look at him. "I thought the party started back at the train station?"

Ben shrugged. "That was the pre-show."

Ashley got the beers.

CHAPTER FIVE

As AJ had predicted, the meat of the journey took about ninety minutes. Ten minutes ago, he had pulled off the motorway, and then the dual carriageway. Now he was turning on to a cracked and dirty B-road. Weeds invaded the tarmac and a pair of twisted steel legs jutted out of the nearby ditch where a road sign would once have stood.

"This is it," said AJ. "I can remember coming down here with my mum as a kid. These trees were all cut back, and there was a big sign with a picture of Alfred the Great on it, holding a big sword."

"Alfred the who?" Ashley asked.

"I dunno," said AJ. "Just some British king from yonks back. I think he beat the Vikings. Anyway, this place used to be themed around ancient Britain. It was all knights and dragons, and stuff like that."

"Shame it's all overgrown," said Samantha as they drove slowly beneath a massive weeping willow. Its tendrils dragged along the glass sunroof like twisting fingernails.

"Okay," said Tasha. "The place looks haunted. Take me home."

Ben downed half of his second beer and groaned. "Try not to embarrass the family name, okay?"

"Our family name is Todd. If I were famous, I'd change it."

AJ watched his friends through the rear-view mirror, switching his attention back and forth between them and the road. Ashley leant forward over the middle seats again, and she patted Ben on the shoulder. "Yeah, *Todd* lacks a certain panache. Sorry, mate."

"Maybe I'll change my name to Wheeler."

Everyone groaned.

AJ slowed the car to a crawl. While Land Rovers were designed for hostile terrain, they were also well known for breaking down, and his was more than a little worse for wear. The bodywork colour could be described as *sun-kissed rust*. With flecks of green.

Overhanging branches encroached on both sides of the road, whipping against the side windows as the car trundled along, and yet the road ahead was surprisingly clear. It narrowed in places as roots tore up its borders, but it managed, for the most part, to remain a road.

"Seriously, guys" – Tasha had her hands on her head and was looking legitimately worried – "we're driving deeper and deeper into the wilderness. Why is no one else freaking out?"

"Because the rest of us are adults," said Ben. "What are you so worried about? This is why we're here. You knew what we had planned. We came here to have fun and make merry. Besides, there's no wilderness in England. You can't go anywhere more than five miles from a road."

Greg raised an eyebrow. "Name your source."

Tasha was still shaking her head. "I just have a sense about these things."

Ben groaned. "Please, sis, don't!"

Ashley chuckled, still leaning over the seat and dangling her long red hair between them. "What? What do you mean, Tasha?"

Tasha looked at Ashley, deadly serious. "I know when something is bad. Like, I can sense evil, you know?"

Greg snorted from Tasha's right. "Christ almighty."

Tasha glared at him. "I'm serious. Last year, I got bad vibes off our neighbour – this skinny dude called Colin. I told Ben he was bad news, but he didn't believe me, just like you don't believe me now. A week after I got those bad vibes, Colin put his ex-girlfriend in hospital and killed himself. Jumped right off the top of the multistorey in town. The Greggs there was closed for three days. People had to go to the one on Arthur Street."

"A tragedy," said Greg, sipping his beer before staring, uninterestedly, out of his window. "The sausage rolls on Arthur Street are always cold."

Samantha turned from the front passenger seat. "I remember that happening. That guy was really your neighbour, Tasha?"

"Yeah, and I knew it was going to happen."

"No, you never," said Ben. "The dude was weird, that's all."

"Lots of people are weird, but only that guy gave me the vibes. The same vibes I'm getting now. Something bad is going to happen."

AJ glanced back at Tasha. She always had been a bit of an oddball, but he'd always put it down to immaturity. Now she was in her mid-twenties, it was starting to be a bit less endearing. "You want me to turn around, T? Like, seriously, do you?"

Tasha chewed her lip for a second, then, "I... well... you

know…" She sighed. "No, if I make us go home, you lot will kill me."

"Too right," said Ben. "Stop acting the tit or you won't be allowed to play with us no more."

Tasha smirked. "Then you'd have to wipe your own arse."

Everyone hooted, but Ben took the jab with a smile. "I think I can manage on my own, thanks, sis. Although I wouldn't mind wiping my shit on your dreads."

Tasha grabbed her dreads and tossed them behind her shoulder. "That's disgusting!"

AJ's gaze flicked forward as something caught his attention. Movement ahead.

He slowed the car.

Shit, is somebody here? Does this place have security? No, no, I've been researching this place for months. It's just a bunch of old metal and cement. Why would anyone guard it?

Samantha noticed AJ staring and shared his concern. "Everything okay?"

"I, um, thought I saw something."

"I thought this place was abandoned," said Greg. "You said we could go wild. Ben was going to fit a nitro tank to his chair."

Ben chuckled.

AJ blinked a few times, making sure his eyes weren't playing tricks on him. Once he was sure they weren't, he sped back up and turned to glance at Greg. "It was probably my imagination. I haven't had a lot of sleep late—"

Samantha screamed. "AJ, stop!"

AJ stamped his foot on the brake and everyone jerked forward. "What the fuck?"

Samantha pointed through the windscreen. "Look!"

A stag stood in the centre of the road, staring right at them. One of its antlers had snapped, almost at the base, and the other seemed ridiculously long, as if to compensate.

"It's a deer," said Samantha, as if she couldn't actually believe it.

AJ stared, eyes glued to the muscular beast blocking their path. While he'd seen the odd deer skipping across country roads on his travels around the country, he'd never seen anything as big as this.

Tasha leant between the two front seats to get a better view through the windscreen. "It's beautiful."

"It is," said Ashley. "Majestic."

"Why is the stupid thing just standing there?" Greg wound down his window and stuck his head out. "Move out the way, you stupid animal."

Ashley punched him in the back of the shoulder. "Don't be a prick. It's got more right to be here than we do."

"Pays its taxes, does it?"

The deer continued to stare at them. It really didn't seem like it planned on moving. AJ wasn't prepared to have a stand-off, too eager to arrive at Saxon Hills, so he took his foot off the brake and rolled the Land Rover forward. The stag held its ground, seeming to glare at him with genuine hatred. Its black eyes smouldered as the swaying branches overhead cast their shifting shadows.

"Are we actually playing a game of chicken with a stag?" asked Ben. "Not where I saw today heading, I have to admit."

"It's not moving," said AJ, gripping the wheel tightly. This had somehow got personal, like the deer was daring him to keep coming.

What was it doing?

Stupid deer.

"Be careful not to hit it," said Samantha.

"I'm not going to hit it," said AJ. "The bloody thing is going to move. Trust me."

Ben was laughing. "It don't look like it plans on moving, mate. Maybe it lost its antler because it does this kind of thing for a hobby. The guardian of the forest."

"Arsehole of the forest more like," muttered Greg.

AJ sat up straight and shifted in his seat. His back was sweating. He was only driving at four miles per hour, but the deer was quickly getting closer. It remained standing in the centre of the road like a statue. The only thing that showed it was alive was the rhythmic clenching of its nostrils. If it didn't move in the next few seconds, there would be a collision. And AJ didn't trust his banged-up Land Rover to come off the better.

The animal snorted. Stood its ground.

"Screw this," said AJ. He stamped his foot down on the accelerator. The ancient three-litre roared.

Samantha looked at him but said nothing.

The distance closed fast. The stag grew massive in the windscreen. Still it stood. Still it stared.

Did it want to die?

Was it mad? Rabid?

The overgrown road got shorter and shorter. The stag was about to meet its end.

You asked for this...
Here it comes...
Nice knowing you, Rudolph!
...Move!
Come on, move!

"Goddammit!" AJ stamped on the brake and yanked up the handbrake. The Land Rover's balding tyres squealed in protest and the entire vehicle lurched sideways. His passengers crashed against one another and cursed his name. AJ's skull thumped back against the headrest and his bad shoulder spiked with pain. His stomach sloshed as the vehicle entered a spin.

Screeech!

The world whizzed by through the windows.

Everything seemed to tilt.

Then the Land Rover came to an abrupt stop, see-sawing on its axles to bleed off the remaining momentum.

Like he did in the ring after taking a bump, AJ remained still for a few seconds, checking nothing was broken. Eventually, he turned to survey his passengers. "Everybody okay?"

Greg looked annoyed, but he nodded.

Tasha, Ben, and Ashley just looked shocked.

"AJ?" Samantha patted him on the arm. "AJ, look!"

She was gawping over his shoulder, looking out of his side window. AJ turned to see what she saw.

The stag was staring right at him through the glass.

AJ threw himself back, hitting his spine on the gearstick and hissing. "What the fuck?"

Greg swore. "What's this thing's problem?"

Tasha leant forward and put a hand on AJ's shoulder, making him flinch. "Get us out of here, AJ. This isn't right."

AJ nodded. "Yeah, I know. Vibes, right?" He wanted to look away from the stag, but he was transfixed – man and beast eye to eye, separated only by a single pane of glass. The Land Rover had stalled, so he carefully put it back in neutral and turned the key. The engine turned over like an old man coughing.

The stag reared up and kicked the side window. The glass pane cracked at its centre, a great radial pattern of sharp lines spreading out towards the frame.

Samantha yelped. Ashley screamed.

AJ swore like he'd never sworn before.

"We're all going to die," cried Ben. "This crazy motherfucker is Cujo."

"Cujo was a dog," said Greg, who refrained from crying out like the rest of them. Despite that, his voice was jittery as he spoke. "Idiot."

Ben shook his head, eyes wide. "Crazy motherfucking *Cujo deer* then. That better?"

"Get us out of here," cried Tasha.

AJ had fumbled the keys when the stag kicked the window, so he had to snap out of his shock to try to start the engine again. This time, he turned the key firmly and didn't let go until the engine rumbled fully to life.

The stag reared and kicked again, this time knocking loose the side mirror. AJ swore, angry that a wild animal was battering his car, but too terrified to do anything but flee. He put the engine in gear and stamped on the accelerator. The Land Rover bucked as the stag reared up and kicked at it a third time.

And then they were shooting forward.

The old Land Rover picked up speed quickly.

The mad beast faded in the rear-view mirror.

"I want to go home," said Tasha. "I told you something bad was going to happen."

"Going home means going past that psychotic animal again." AJ looked in the rear-view mirror. The stag was just standing there, watching them speed away. What the hell had just happened? "Let's put some distance between us and it. Then we can take a breather and figure out what to do."

Greg was laughing, despite nobody else finding the situation funny. "We got our arses handed to us by a deer. Seriously, does anybody understand what just happened and how crazy it is?"

After a while, relief set in and everyone tittered

nervously. Even AJ found it funny, forgetting the damage to his car and the pain in his shoulder. He had wanted to create memories this weekend, and in that regard things were going well. *Don't think any of us will ever forget crazy motherfucking Cujo deer.*

What the hell?

CHAPTER SIX

"Maybe we should call someone," said Ashley. Everyone had their seatbelts off now, moving around the Land Rover's cabin as though it was a cramped sitting room. Ashley was handing out fresh beers, which they all needed after what had happened.

AJ shook his head in disbelief. *Attacked by a stag. Oh, the humiliation.*

Greg turned back to face Ashley. "Who can we call?"

She shrugged. "The police? We were just attacked. There's a wild animal on the loose."

"Yeah, a wild animal loose in the countryside miles from anywhere. I think the stag was pretty much doing what it's allowed to do. We're the ones planning a weekend of raising hell."

"I don't know about that," said Ben. "Deer aren't usually aggressive, are they? I mean, I never had to watch any educational videos on deer attacks when I was a kid. It was all 'stranger danger' and don't walk on the train tracks – although I probably could've called in sick that day."

"It's probably mating season," said Samantha. "Stags are territorial, aren't they?"

Greg chuckled. "Maybe it thought AJ's scrapheap of a car was a deer, huh? It's covered in dirt and smells like shit. You can see the confusion."

AJ rolled his eyes. "Remind me why I'm friends with you again, Greg?"

"Because I'm the best personal trainer you ever met, and you would still be a sweaty tub of lard without me."

AJ gave a laugh. While it was a slight over-exaggeration, three years ago, Greg had indeed helped him drop another four per cent body fat after his training regime had plateaued. His wrestling career had received a boost as he'd gone from fit and athletic to toned and muscular.

"Maybe he wanted you for your discounted gym memberships," said Tasha. "Hey, by the way, I'm still waiting for mine."

"I only get so many a year," Greg replied, "and they go to my friends in order of how much I like them. You should get yours in about... oh, I don't know, six years or so."

Tasha whacked him on one of his huge biceps. "Dick!"

"So, are we going to call someone or not?" Ashley asked again. "You guys don't think we need to?"

Ben slid his phone out of his breast pocket. "Let me have a butcher's online. Okay, *what to do when attacked by an antisocial deer*... Ah, shit, no signal."

AJ looked back. "Really? We must really be in the sticks. I reckon we've been on this road for about a mile now. We should be at the park any minute."

"I've got no signal either," said Ashley. "Are we still planning on going through with this after what happened? I never signed up for no phone signal. How am I supposed to Instagram?"

Greg groaned. "It'll do you good to be away from your phone for a couple of days. The world will cope without seeing you pout every time you eat a carrot stick."

Tasha gasped. "Ashley, you have such a loving boyfriend."

"She likes the abuse," said Greg. "Treat 'em mean, keep 'em keen."

AJ looked in the rear-view and saw Ashley pull a face. Then she smiled. "I give as good as I get. He's just lucky he's got a fat cock."

Ben gagged on a mouthful of beer. "Whoa, no one needs to hear that shit, Ashley. There's a reason men wear pants, and trust me, it's not out of respect for women. It's so blokes don't have to look at other bloke's junk."

AJ tuned out his friends' banter. The road was ending up ahead, and he needed to concentrate. It felt as though he was driving in the dark, the tree canopy now so thick that it was nearly a solid roof. The bushes and overgrowth had also thickened, obscuring a majority of the road. Branches cracked beneath the Land Rover's wheels like gunfire.

Samantha was focusing ahead. "Is there a way forward? Looks a bit perilous."

AJ shrugged. "We must be near the park now. Maybe we'll have to get out and walk the last bit."

"Yeah, um, okay. Long as there are no more deer."

The stretch of road they were about to hit was cracked so badly that it was more mud than tarmac, and it forced AJ to warn the others. "Going off-road!"

Everyone bounced in their seats as the Land Rover hit a dip, and AJ enjoyed a secret smile as the car rocked around like an old stagecoach. Ben cried out in protest as his wheelchair knocked against his chest, but everyone else was smiling and having a good time.

They bounced along for several minutes, whooping with

every bump and dip, and AJ was cackling by the time the road smoothed out and became tarmac again. The trees and bushes fell away and the way ahead became clear.

They had arrived.

The Land Rover entered an overgrown car park resembling a setting from a post-apocalyptic movie – cement, grass, and memories of what came before. A variety of signage hung from steel posts at various angles, but most were obscured by dirt and foliage. At the far side of the car park, a hundred metres back at least, was a wide chain-link fence. Beyond it, the towering shadows of several mysterious structures loomed.

"Wow," said Samantha. "We're actually here. Look at this place. It's like a secret world."

"It's a car park," said Greg. "Brilliant."

"Nah, man," said Ben. "This is actually pretty cool. How often do you get to go somewhere without other people? You could die here and no one would find your body for years – maybe not ever. I don't know about you, but I'm going to be watching my step."

AJ laughed. "Yeah, you don't want to end up in a wheelchair."

"Can we find a parking space?" Ashley asked sarcastically. "Or is it too busy?"

"Don't worry," said Tasha. "My brother's here, we can park in the disabled."

AJ drove across the car park, surrounded by hundreds of spaces on all sides. He didn't think he'd need to squeeze in anywhere today. Maybe the weekend was still salvageable. "I'll pull up as close to the park as I can and then—" He lurched in his seat as the steering wheel went stiff in his hands. The Land Rover bucked like it had driven over loose bricks. AJ swore in surprise.

"What the...?" Greg had tumbled into the footwell, his beer spilling everywhere.

"We hit something!" said Ashley.

AJ wasn't so sure. "No, I think..." He punched the steering wheel. "I think we punctured a tyre."

Everyone groaned.

AJ brought them to a careful halt in one of the spaces – not that he needed to be courteous of other drivers – then switched off the engine. He pulled the handbrake and climbed out of the car to inspect the damage. Greg got out behind him. Both of them were silent.

Eventually, Greg asked a question. "Is that... Is that what I think it is?"

AJ nodded. "Yeah, it is."

It made no sense, but somehow they had driven right over a long, bony antler. Like the kind you would find on a reindeer, or a large, angry stag.

CHAPTER SEVEN

AJ AND GREG stood staring at the antler for a full minute before the others grew curious enough to get out and investigate for themselves. Samantha came up alongside AJ and fell to stunned silence with him. Tasha helped Ben climb into his chair and then wheeled him around with Ashley. They saw the antler at the same time.

Tasha freaked out. "I told you we should've turned around. This place isn't right."

Greg shook his head and sighed. "What, it's haunted by a mad deer, is it? It's just a coincidence."

"Hell of a coincidence," said Ben, pulling on a pair of stylish green-and-black sports gloves. "I think we get the tyre changed and call this weekend a bust. Sorry, AJ, I know this meant a lot to you."

AJ opened his mouth to speak, but Tasha spoke over him. "Yes! We should leave. I don't want to be here."

AJ ground his teeth, dumbfounded that they had been cursed by such shit luck. He put his hands on his hips and faced the others. "Come on, guys. Don't freak out on me, please. It's just a flat tyre. Nobody's hurt, are they? The only damage is to my car. Let's just have fun like we planned."

Greg put his hands on his hips, mirroring AJ. "Sorry, mate, but I think I'm going to have to agree. While I don't for one second think this place is haunted" – he side-eyed Tasha – "I don't think this weekend was meant to be. It's gone from bad to worse, and honestly, I always thought the whole thing was a bit stupid anyway. Let's just get your car roadworthy, and we'll have a night down the pub back home, yeah?"

AJ didn't want to say what he was about to say. He could see how on edge his friends were and he didn't want to make things worse. There was a very real chance they might try to hurt him once he told them what he was about to. "I don't have a spare."

Greg frowned, then chuckled, then scowled. "What? How? How... How do you not have a spare? Are you serious?"

"There's one here," said Ashley, pointing, "hanging off the back of the car."

AJ cleared his throat, a pit forming in his stomach. "That's not the spare. I've actually been driving on the spare. The one on the back is an old tyre some crazy fan slashed about nine months ago after a show."

"For crying out loud." Greg kicked the pavement, sending up a cloud of dust. "Are you an idiot or what? You bring us out in the middle of nowhere without a spare? You've had nine months to get one."

"I didn't think about it. Nobody expects to get a flat, do they?"

Samantha leant back against the car and sighed. "Wow, this is bad."

"Has anybody got any signal at all?" Ashley looked from

face to face. "We're going to need to call the AA or something."

"Yeah," said Greg, running a hand over his shaved head, "and explain that we're parked outside a theme park that's been closed for a decade."

Everyone checked their phones. No one had a signal.

Tasha paced the car park. "I'm having really bad vibes here, guys. Real bad."

Ben reached out and grabbed her wrist, not hard, but gently – a reassuring gesture. "Chill out, sis. We're fine."

"We're *not* fine. We shouldn't be here."

"Sis, just calm—"

Tasha broke free of her brother's grip and paced away from the group. She pulled out her phone and held it up in front of her face, waving it back and forth as if getting a signal was merely reliant upon finding some hidden air pocket.

Ashley chased after her. "Hey, don't rush off. We'll figure this out, okay, but let's take a second."

"We need to leave," Tasha shouted back at her in a panic. This place is freaking me out."

Ashley hurried to catch up. "Tasha, just wait! There's no reason to freak ou— argh!" Ashley collapsed to the pavement and grabbed her ankle.

Tasha was still ranting, but when she heard Ashley cry out in pain, she turned and rushed back to help. AJ hurried too, and they reached her at the same time. AJ undid Ashley's laces before swelling set in. "What happened?"

Ashely pointed, teeth clenched in pain. "A bloody – ah, shite, it hurts – a bloody pothole."

"I'm so sorry," said Tasha.

AJ studied the ground nearby and saw a patch of uneven concrete. "You rolled your ankle, Ash. Does it feel broken?"

"I don't know! Jeez, it hurts."

"Move aside," said Greg irritably as he came over. He knelt beside Ashley and elevated her ankle. Then he removed her trainer and sock. The elastic had left embedded lines in her pale flesh. "Can you move it?"

Ashley whimpered, but she managed to rotate her ankle and wiggle her tiny orange-painted toes. "Yeah, I don't think it's broken."

Greg gave a satisfied grunt. "It's just a sprain. You'll be fine. Try to keep your weight off it."

AJ sat on the floor next to her. "This is turning into a disaster."

Greg rolled his eyes. "No shit."

"It's not AJ's fault," said Ashley between hisses of pain. "Bad luck is nobody's fault. Just help me up and stop being a grumpy arse."

Greg huffed, but he helped her up. Tasha took Ashley's other arm, and the two of them carried her back over to the Land Rover.

Samantha hopped up on the bonnet and began tapping her boot heels against the top of the tyre. "So what do we do? We can't drive out of here and we can't call anyone."

"We'll have to go for help," said Ben. "I know we're a bit isolated, but it's not like we're in the middle of the desert. We can probably make it back to the road in an hour or two."

"There's a problem with that," said Greg. He pointed at the punctured tyre and the crushed antler poking out from beneath it. "There's a rabid stag back the way we came. Anyone fancy a stroll through its territory?"

"And it's getting dark," said Samantha, looking up at the greying sky.

"I'm not walking back through the woods in the dark,"

said Ashley. "I don't even think I can. My ankle is killing me."

"So what then?" asked Ben, rubbing his forehead like he had a headache coming on. "I want to hear a plan here, guys. I'll be honest, I don't usually let being in a wheelchair hold me back, but I draw the line at wilderness survival. You people have forced me to it, I'm playing my disability card." He pretended to slap a card down on his knee.

"We can keep trying our phones," said Ashley. "I'm sure we'll get a signal eventually."

"Why?" asked Greg. "You think one of the masts will suddenly move closer?"

"Fuck you. Will you stop being such a miserable bastard?"

Greg folded his arms, tutted, then turned away to lean against the Land Rover's boxy rear end – a grown man in a tiny vest sulking. AJ groaned. No one was having fun.

This mess was all down to him. *His* passion had led them there, his love of theme parks and their history.

I should have known they wouldn't enjoy it. Nobody enjoys this stuff but me. It's just... a person only has so long to see things. I wanted to see this place.

I made it so close.

None of his friends had wanted to come when he'd first suggested the trip – *urban exploring*, he'd called it to make it sound more legitimate – but he'd chipped away at them until they'd relented. He had dragged them away from their sensible, grown-up lives to go camping at an abandoned slab of concrete in the middle of nowhere. Brilliant.

Ashley grabbed a beer from the car and started necking it. If there was such a thing as *angry drinking*, then she was doing it.

"We can still make the best of this," AJ said, realising he

sounded desperate. "Look, it's getting too dark to head out for the main road, and with that stag on the loose, it wouldn't be safe either. We brought beer, camping equipment, and enough snacks to give an elephant diabetes. Let's just do what we came here to do and have some fun. In the morning, Greg and I will set off to find help. We made it here, didn't we, so let's enjoy ourselves."

Ben shrugged. "I suppose we could do that. All that's happened, really, is that we're a bit stranded, but at least we're stranded in the place we planned on being, right? Besides, if we try to get help now, it'll end up being the middle of the night by the time we get home. I'd rather sort things out in the morning."

Relief flooded through AJ. He hadn't expected to find an ally so easily. But then Greg ruined it all. "I never wanted to do this thing anyway," he said, "and now I'm not in the mood at all. You lot stay here. I'll head out and bring back a mechanic to fix AJ's shitheap of a car."

Ashley hobbled over to him. "You can't head out on your own, Greg. It's not safe. Don't leave me here."

"She's right," said Tasha. She'd been standing in silence for a few minutes, but now she was animated again. "We need to stay together. I strongly believe that we need to stay together."

Greg looked at them like a bunch of misbehaving children. "You lot are ridiculous. I'll jog it. We'll probably be back on the road in two hours."

"Please," said AJ, surprising himself by his own desperate plea, but once it was out there, he went with it. He was prepared to beg. It meant that much to him. "I'm leaving, Greg. Like, *for good* leaving. And soon."

"You're leaving?" Samantha hopped off the bonnet and stood in front of him. "Going away?"

AJ spoke directly to her while the others listened. "Yeah, I um... I got offered a developmental deal with the big leagues. I head to America next month. If all goes well, I won't be coming back."

Everyone fell silent, and AJ realised they were working through their disbelief. They knew he was a good wrestler, had each watched him in several matches, but those matches had been in front of tiny crowds at bingo halls and local theatres. They were struggling to equate him with the massive arena spectacles of prime time professional wrestling that had launched household names like The Rock and Hulk Hogan.

Samantha seemed the most stunned. "Are you... are you serious?"

He nodded. "Yeah."

She shocked him with an outburst. "Oh my God, oh my God, oh my God. That's incredible! I always knew you'd make it." She grabbed him in a massive hug and squeezed.

"Argh, easy. My shoulder, remember?"

She let go. "Sorry!"

Ben wheeled himself over to AJ, a big smile on his face. "That's amazing, man. Good going!"

"Awesome," Tasha gave him a high five. "Wish I was going to America. I'm excited for you."

"Don't forget us when you're famous," said Ashley.

Greg was the only one not to congratulate him. In fact, he appeared suspicious. "I was talking to Tractor on Tuesday. He never mentioned anything about you getting a contract."

AJ nodded. "Oh, um, yeah, well, I haven't mentioned it to him yet. We kind of had a falling out."

"Yeah, he *did* tell me about *that*. Said you decked him in the ring and injured Dillon, who, incidentally, is booked in for two months of physio with me, so thanks for that. Dillon said you totally missed a catch and dropped him."

Guilt struck AJ like a slap on the back of the head. Dillon had suffered a major fracture of the ulna bone in his forearm caused by his awkward landing. AJ had taken him out of the game for at least three months, maybe longer. He'd taken away the guy's ability to earn. What made things even worse was the fact that Dillon had been so forgiving about it all. *I know you, AJ. You're one of the safest hands in the business. You just had a bad night. We're okay, brother. It's all good.*

"Dillon and I squared things," said AJ, "but I feel bad enough without you going on about it. Look, you lot are my best mates. I can't leave without having one last hurrah with you all. So, please, stay. Let me have this?"

"Have what?" asked Ben. "What do you want us to do?"

"Exactly what we all planned to do. We grab our gear and find a way into Saxon Hills. We drink, eat, and talk about the old times until we pass out. There'll be plenty of time to work out a way home tomorrow, but tonight can still be a laugh. Haven't you all missed this? Hanging out and doing dumb shit like we used to? When did we get so old?"

Ben sighed, but nodded. "Have to admit, spending all week in an office isn't the life I dreamed of."

"I'm happy to stay," said Samantha, putting a hand on AJ's arm. "We need to celebrate your good news." She glared at Greg. "We all do."

AJ wanted to kiss her then, but he chose to focus on the person who would swing the vote – Greg.

Greg folded his arms and grunted. "Yeah, well, I don't see what choice there is. First thing in the morning though, I'm setting off."

AJ nodded and offered a handshake. "Thanks, man. I'm sorry, okay?"

Greg finally let his bad attitude fade and shook AJ's hand, but he broke away and went over to the Land Rover. He opened the rear door and started handing out beers. "Let's carb up, kids. Here's to AJ! The next Stone Cold Steve Armstrong."

"Austin," AJ corrected, but nobody else seemed to care. For a guy that worked in the business, he knew shit-all about the history of wrestling.

Everyone grabbed a beer and, all of a sudden, everything was fine. They were all having fun again.

Although AJ found it hard to smile.

This would likely be the last time he saw them together like this. The last chance at making memories he could hold on to. He was going to miss them.

He held up his beer. "To me!"

CHAPTER EIGHT

Greg and AJ bore most of the weight on their shoulders, rucksacks full of beer, wine, and snacks. Everyone else wore smaller backpacks, stuffed with sleeping bags and smaller camping supplies. Ashley had an additional hip bag that housed her camera and lenses, but she refused to give it up despite hobbling along on a sprained ankle.

They shuffled across the dilapidated car park towards the chain-link fence. An entrance area broke up its centre, but the structure there had long ago been boarded up. A pair of castle turrets rose either side of a rusty row of turnstiles, and a thick wall of plywood had been erected behind. The bottom of the turrets housed small offices with planked-up windows. Ticket offices.

"I remember being here as a kid," said AJ. "My mum was a total wimp when it came to rides, but she always brought me here at least once a year until she... well, you know?"

Everyone nodded and gave thin-lipped smiles. They all knew his mum well, having crashed at his house regularly during their party days. At twenty-nine, AJ's mother had been diagnosed with *Leber's hereditary optic neuropathy*. By thirty-two, she had been almost completely blind. AJ had been eleven, and in the space of a few years, he'd gone from being a child to a full-time carer. His mother hadn't been born blind, which meant she was incapable at first, unable to cook or clean. Unable to read. She relied on him for everything. His mum had ceased to exist, as she became, instead, a burden, a chore. It was some time before she became a person again. A long time before her depression finally lifted. By the time AJ had a mother again, he was a fully grown man no longer in need of one.

"How is your mum?" asked Ashley. She, in particular, had always got along well with his mother. They shared a love of Motown music and crappy Saturday night singing shows – one of the few kinds of shows his mum could still enjoy after going blind.

"She's doing good," said AJ. "She still works part-time at the private school. Keeps her occupied."

"Tell her I said hi."

AJ smiled. "Will do."

"So how do we get inside?" asked Tasha. She was looking around nervously, as though she expected the crazed stag to suddenly appear and charge them. She had ceased alarming everyone with her 'bad vibes', but she was still clearly anxious. "The entrance building is all boarded up. We'd need a bulldozer to get through it."

"We're going to make our own entrance," said AJ with a wink. He'd already thought about this.

Greg shifted the weight on his shoulders. "What do you mean?"

AJ picked up his pace so he reached the chain-link fence first. Once there, he knelt and shrugged off his rucksack. Among the beer cans and wine bottles was a cloth bag full of tools. He pulled out the tool he needed and showed it to the others.

"Wow," said Samantha. "You really thought this through, didn't you?"

AJ snapped the bolt cutters open and closed like a piranha's mouth. "I wish I could say this is my first time breaking in somewhere."

Samantha giggled. "You reprobate."

AJ stooped in front of the fence and positioned the cutters around one of the links. "Three... two... one!"

Clip.

The link snipped apart easily, and it was oddly satisfying. AJ got to work cutting out an entrance in the fence, and it was only a few minutes more before he had made a gap big enough to push a trolley through.

"Those things are great," said Ben. "I bet they could take a finger right off."

Tasha groaned. "Don't tempt fate."

Ben rolled his eyes. "You still freaking out on us? Just chill, sis."

"I'm okay," she said, not looking okay at all. "I just want everyone to be careful. Haunted or not, this place is probably dangerous."

"She's right," said Greg. "We already have one casualty. Let's watch our step and make sure we don't do anything stupid. Don't forget, this entire place has been condemned."

AJ packed away his bolt cutters and knelt in front of the opening. "I'll go first. That way, if anyone gets impaled, it'll be me."

"Sounds like a plan," said Greg.

Tasha shook her head in disapproval. "You keep tempting fate, and that's exactly what'll happen."

"There's no such thing as fate," said Ben.

But as AJ passed through the gap in the fence, he couldn't help thinking to himself, *Oh, yes, there is. And you can't escape it.*

CHAPTER NINE

IT WAS everything AJ had hoped for. While most of the rides had been removed, a few – obviously the ones no other parks had wanted – still stood in place. The structures had ceased being man-made creations and were now ancient, unmovable monoliths. Features of the landscape, like mountains or giant oak trees.

"This spot!" said AJ, pointing down at a massive slab of discoloured concrete beneath his feet. "This is where the *Crown Fall* used to be. It was a thirty-foot Vekoma parachute tower. You could see it rising up from the car park like a great big welcome. An amusement company in Wales has it now on a pier."

Greg kicked at the ground, dislodging weeds and dirt. A huge steel bolt jutted from the pavement. "How do you know all this stuff? You're like a kid."

AJ felt his cheeks heat up. "I know it's nerdy, but I just love theme parks. Whenever I wrestle up and down the country, I always check out the local attractions. It makes every long, arduous journey something to look forward to. I must have ridden the Big One at Blackpool twenty times, and there's this place down in Dartmouth with these fantastic waterslides that I could ride all day long. I love discovering them all. Especially the rides few people know about."

Greg scrunched up his nose. "Really? I don't see the attraction – excuse the pun."

"That's because most people go on rides without giving them any consideration beyond the thirty seconds they're on them, but so much goes into designing them and building them." AJ felt himself getting excited, and he tried to keep his voice at a reasonable volume. "And they're always changing. Rides evolve. Do you know the *Lilo & Stitch* ride at Disney's Magic Kingdom was originally intended to be based on the *Alien* franchise? It got changed for being too scary. It's common knowledge."

"It's *not* common knowledge," said Greg. "Not for anyone normal."

AJ gave Greg the finger. "There's more to life than shifting weight, you know?"

"No, there is literally only shifting weight. Go hard or go home. That's my entire credo."

"Which is funny for a guy who can't get it up some nights," said Ashley with a smirk.

Greg seemed miffed by the jab as everyone hooted in laughter. He shot Ashley a glare but eventually chose to shrug off the insult and laugh along with them. AJ wondered if Ashley had really been joking, or making a complaint. More likely the beers back at the car had just gone to her head.

Greg and Ashley had been together for over two years, ever since meeting at one of AJ's wrestling events. After Greg had helped him in the gym, AJ had got him a side gig as a personal trainer for a wrestling promotion – Tractor's promotion – which was why he often attended the shows. Therefore, AJ took credit for the two of them getting together.

"What did that used to be?" Tasha pointed to a twisted pillar of melted plastic about three feet high.

AJ shrugged. "Looks like someone set fire to a bin. Behind it though, that crumbling brick wall used to be a block of toilets."

Tasha raised an eyebrow at him. "Fascinating."

"It's nearly dark," said Samantha, glancing at her watch and then up at the sky. "Almost seven. We need to find a place to camp."

"Yeah," said Ben, rubbing at his arms. "Getting chilly too. Couldn't we have done this in the summer?"

AJ nodded. Of course he didn't expect them to bed down on the concrete. He knew what was here – had been researching the place for years. "When the park closed," he said, "they sold off most the rides, either intact or stripped for copper and lead, etcetera, but there were a few structures that got left behind, including a restaurant called the *Great Hunt*. The building was constructed to resemble a Viking longhouse, and it was made mostly from timber, which isn't worth much recycled. I thought we could camp there."

"Sounds good to me," said Ben. "Always fancied myself as a Viking. I'd be great at rowing the seven seas." He pinwheeled his arms.

Greg laughed. "What, because of all the wanking you do?"

Ben flexed his fists. "I do whatever I have to do to amuse myself."

"Okay," said Ashley. "I'd really like to get off this ankle, so lead the way, AJ."

AJ nodded and headed off. It was strange, but he

would've known his way around better if the maze of rides and facilities still existed. The flat, weed-strewn pavement clashed with his memory of the place as a child, and it left him disorientated. In some places, the grass had grown so long through the pavement that it looked like a meadow.

A slope rose ahead, gentle but long. They had to go slow for both Ashley and Ben, but when they reached the top, the park grew more impressive.

The log flume was the tallest remaining structure, its tandem drops and various tunnels snaking together like a complicated knot, and it stood proud on the horizon. Equally impressive was the narrow stream that ran in a perfect line across the top of the slope. A pair of wooden bridges spanned it, sixty metres apart, but the white picket fence running alongside had snapped and broken in places, and its chipped paintwork gave way to greens and greys.

Ashley limped along. "Are those bridges safe?"

AJ shrugged. How would he know simply by looking at them? "I'm sure they're fine, but even if not, that stream's a foot deep. It's not like you'll be swept away."

Greg went up to the nearest bridge and prodded at the boards with his trainer. "It's fine," he said. "Hurry up."

AJ grabbed Ben's wheelchair and rushed him forward, much to his protest. "Hey, man! Think I'm just going to sit here and let you push me around?"

"Yeah," said AJ. "I do."

He picked up speed, tipping the chair into a wheelie. Ben's protests turned to laughter, and when they hit the foot of the bridge, the chair hopped a little and gained a couple of inches of air.

"Be careful," Tasha shouted after them. "You break him, you buy him."

"I won't break him," said AJ as they hit the peak of the bridge. "I'm just having a little bit of— Shit!"

Tasha cried out and started running. "What is it?"

AJ cackled. He had pretended to crash Ben's chair into the hedges, but instead spun him around at the last second. Ben was cursing, but giggling too. Once Tasha realised it was a joke, she had some choice words to offer.

"That's strike one, AJ."

"Duly noted."

They all made it across the bridge in one piece, and AJ led them towards where he remembered the *Great Hunt* being. He thought he saw it ahead, but something wasn't quite right. He expected a long, wooden structure, but they were heading towards a blackened husk.

"What *is* that?" Samantha tilted her head, ponytail flopping against her shoulder. "It looks burnt."

"It is," said Greg. "Someone torched whatever this was. This isn't the restaurant you were talking about, is it?"

AJ sighed. The closer they got, the surer he became that, yes, this was indeed the remains of what had once been the *Great Hunt*.

A collection of fake shields lay in a pile, their steel facades blackened but unmelted. A severed head in a horned helmet lay on its side, staring at them through melted plastic eyes. The stench of charcoal and burning still clung to the air, even with the fire long dead.

"I think this was it," said AJ, wishing it wasn't so. He'd based the whole camping weekend on there being at least one habitable building to sleep in. "It was left standing when the park closed. Someone must have set fire to it since. Bloody vandals."

"So we're not the first to come here exploring," said Greg. "Guess that means we won't be planting any flags."

Ben rolled over to the building's scorched remains and studied them with interest. "If this building's been torched, what are they odds the others have been too?"

"We can try the log flume entrance," said AJ, trying to think fast. "It's an enclosed cabin. Not that big, but it should be secure. Come on, it's at the back of the park."

"Oh, great," said Ashley. "More walking."

Greg put his arm around her waist and let her lean on him. "We need to rest Ash's ankle or it'll swell up like a piss-filled condom. What if we get to this log flume and it's burnt down too?"

AJ could see Ashley was in pain – he had strapped up enough of his own sprains to know how agonising it could be. They couldn't keep dragging her around. "Okay," he said, "there's one other place we could go, but you won't like it. Should be right over there..." He pointed to a dense grouping of nearby trees. It had been a landscaped area once, erected to form Pagan's Grove – a mock clearing in the middle of the woods – but it had now grown wild. A handful of rides had been erected in the grove area, but only one now remained. And it was notorious.

"Where are you thinking?" asked Ben.

AJ sighed and came out with it. "Frenzy. It's a dark ride, so the whole thing is under a roof. If we can get inside, it'll make the perfect place to camp out for the night."

"No way," said Tasha. "You're talking about the ride that killed a bunch of people?"

"A madman with a blowtorch and petrol killed a bunch of people. The ride just made it hard for them to get out."

Tasha folded her arms and looked away in disgust. "Oh, that's *so* much better."

Greg spoke next. "If it burned down, how is it supposed to be a good place to camp out?"

AJ sighed. "I already told you. After the fire, it was quickly rebuilt and made safe. The owners couldn't afford to lose the money they had invested into the ride so they reopened it. When the park closed, Frenzy was still fully operational."

"Then why didn't anyone buy it?" asked Samantha.

"Dark rides are hard to resituate because so much of their theming is tied to the building they are housed in. But the main reason no one wanted to buy Frenzy is because nine people died inside it."

"Makes perfect sense to me," said Ben. "Nobody wants to go on a death ride."

"And we'd have to be crazy to camp inside one as well," said Tasha. "It's a bad idea."

AJ sighed. "Why? Because you actually believe in ghosts and monsters? I mean, come on."

Tasha was breathing heavily, and it was unclear whether she was panicking or just annoyed. "You don't mess around with places like that. That ride has bad memories attached to it, and bad memories can bite your hand off if you don't pay them enough respect."

"I have to admit," said Ashley, "the thought of staying in a ride where people died is a bit much for me as well."

"That's why it'll be exciting," said Greg, looking at Ashley like he enjoyed the thought of her being afraid. Then he looked at AJ. "Right?"

AJ felt embarrassed and stared down at the ground. "Well, yeah, part of me would like to do it for the experience. People stay in supposedly haunted places all the time, don't they? I guess it's something on my bucket list. I never planned on camping inside Frenzy this weekend, but seeing it at least is one of the main reasons I'm here. It's part of the park's history. Theme park history."

Samantha turned to him. "This is important to you?"

He thought for a moment and then nodded. "I think so, yeah."

"Okay" – she cleared her throat – "then I'm in. I'm probably going to wet my pants, but I'll try to remind myself that I'm an adult, and that ghosts and goblins don't exist."

"I used to love that game," said Ben. "If you got hit, you ended up in your underpants."

Greg folded his arms and shrugged his massive traps – like the hood of a cobra. "It sounds better than spending the night in a rusty old log flume, so I'm game too. This thing will have doors, I assume? And a roof?"

AJ nodded. "The whole ride is enclosed. It should be the warmest place in the park."

"Then I'm in too," said Ben. "I don't enjoy being cold. My people hail from warmer climates."

Ashley looked confused. "I thought your family were from Birmingham."

"Yes, but believe it or not we are not ethnically Brummie. My grandparents were from Trinidad."

Ashley blushed. "Oh. Well, okay then, I'll do whatever the group decides. I just don't want to walk any more."

Tasha was tapping her foot on the ground, fidgeting like she was covered in ants. "I'm not going inside that ride. No way."

"Where else are you going to go then, sis?" Ben wheeled around to face her. "It's almost dark, and it's getting cold. You can either stick things out with the rest of us, or go find some place on your own. You're acting like a kid. We can't keep making Ashley walk around on her ankle. She's suffering. I want to relax and have some beers, not roll around a bunch of concrete all night."

Tasha glanced at Ashley, who gave her a small, pleading

nod. *Just say yes*, she seemed to be saying. Eventually, Tasha hissed and stamped her foot. "Okay, fine, but promise me we'll leave at the first sign of... *anything*."

"We promise." AJ knew he was beaming like a clown, but he couldn't help himself. This was really happening. They were going to spend the night inside Frenzy. "First sign of a ghost and I'll be right behind you."

"You'll be right *beneath* me," Tasha told him. "I'll trample your pasty white ass."

AJ nodded. "Fair enough. Come on, it's this way."

CHAPTER TEN

Ashley was really struggling with her ankle. AJ took Greg's rucksack so he could give his girlfriend a piggyback. She would be limping for a few days at least.

"Is it much further?" asked Greg, probably because he disliked having to carry Ashley rather than because he was struggling with her weight. He was one of the strongest people AJ knew – and he knew some pretty gigantic guys – but he wasn't the most accommodating of boyfriends. No such thing as chivalry in the twenty-first century, he would often say to female wrestlers when they begged him for a break from his backbreaking workout routines. Suzy Shakedown, a green-eared trainee, had once punched him on the nose before quitting the company altogether. She had been no great loss, admittedly, but most people thought Greg had deserved it. Compassion wasn't his strong suit.

"It's just inside these trees," said AJ. "The whole area is meant to be like a pagan settlement. Saxon Hills was themed around the Viking invasion of Britain. Christianity was still spreading at that time, so some people still worshipped the old gods, like Woden."

"You're not a normal wrestler, are you?" said Ben. "I've met some of the sweaty dudes you grapple with and most of them still struggle with the alphabet."

AJ chuckled. It was nice that Ben, in a backhanded kind of way, was calling him smart, and it was true that AJ enjoyed educating himself, but he had chosen to be a wrestler because he loved it, not because he was witless. "It's a mixture," he said. "Some of the guys I've worked with have day jobs as accountants and teachers, while others sofa hop their entire lives without ever doing a proper day's work. The call of the squared circle entices all souls."

"Okay," said Greg impatiently, "so where in Woden's grove are we heading?"

"I think we're already here," said Samantha. "Guys, look at that!"

AJ had seen pictures of Frenzy's entrance on the Internet, but seeing it for real was a different experience. It was like nothing he had ever seen before. The dark ride had opened after his mother's blindness, which was why he had never ridden it, but now he was finally here, standing before it.

The giant bronze helmet was a looming presence poking out from between a pair of slanting elm trees. Weeds, moss, and creeping ivy covered its surface, which made it seem menacing and ancient. Both horns were still intact, stabbing at the darkening sky.

"I am not going in there," said Tasha. "It looks evil."

"It's *supposed* to look evil," said Greg, "but it's just a bunch of steel and fibreglass."

Ashley slid down from Greg's back and then leant against him. "Sorry, guys, I'm with Tasha. I don't think I can go in there."

AJ tried to put his hand on Ashley's back, but he

couldn't get past all of her thick red hair. "Greg's right. It looks scary because it was built to look scary. It's a thrill ride."

"Yes, I know that, but it's also an evil helmet in the middle of nowhere, guarding a place where people died. It's freaky."

"It's cool," said Ben. "It better have wheelchair access."

Tasha was rooted to the spot. "Seriously, guys…"

Samantha started forward. "The sooner we go inside, the sooner it will stop being scary. Come on, let's just get it over with."

AJ and Greg gave each other a look, and AJ chuckled. "Looks like it's ladies first."

Samantha chuckled too, even as she continued moving forward. "I fell off a horse when I was a kid, almost as soon as I started riding. My mum told me to get straight back on because the best way to stop being scared of something is to become master of it. If something scares you, don't just face it, own it. So, yeah, let's get inside this ride and then we can stop being scared of it. Once we see the nuts and bolts sticking out of the floor, we'll realise it's just a building pretending to be something else."

Ashley continued moaning, but peer pressure moved her forward. Greg put an arm around her and helped her walk on her bad ankle. Tasha got moving too, but stayed completely silent, playing nervously with her dreads. AJ was glad everyone was still onboard, but he was concerned about anyone else getting hurt. He jogged to the front of the pack, intending to lead the way – intending to take on any dangers himself.

He never expected to slip.

"Whoa!" He swung his arms out and just managed to keep his balance as his legs splayed.

Samantha grimaced and turned her head away. "Ew, that's disgusting!"

AJ looked at his foot and almost gagged. He was unsure what he'd stepped in, but it might once have been alive. In fact, he was fairly certain he felt bones crunch beneath his heel.

"Looks like a dead fox or something," said Greg.

"Now it's blood and fur cheesecake," said Ben, wheeling his chair in a wide arc to avoid the remains.

AJ went and wiped his boot on some weeds growing through the pavement, but he knew the stains on the tan leather would be permanent. "Okay, everyone, watch your step."

"Bit late for that," said Greg. "Come on, let's find a way in."

AJ went with Greg towards the large Viking helmet. AJ couldn't resist dropping another info bomb on his friends. "Do you know that Vikings never actually had horns on their helmets? It's an invention of modern media."

"Television makes everything cooler," said Greg. "I bet the battles were a hell of a lot duller in real life too."

AJ nodded. "We're lucky to live in a time where we have theme parks and cheap flights instead of conscription and the plague."

Greg kicked at a broken piece of wood, then turned on AJ and pretended to swipe at him with a sword. "Have to admit, it would've been cool to be a warrior or a knight. The amount of times I'd have liked to lop some twat's head off. Or stick a sword in Tractor's big fat guts. I'd have made an awesome knight. Greg the Granite Knight."

AJ pretended to defend and parry with his own imaginary sword, but couldn't help but laugh. "Yeah, it'd be all fun and games until someone stuck an axe in your face. Think

I'll stick to fake fighting in the ring, thanks. All the fun with none of the being dead."

"Well, that depends on who you're relying on to catch you after leaping the top rope."

AJ stopped making slashing motions and stood up straight. He frowned at Greg. "That's not funny, man. Do you have any idea how badly I feel about what happened? I take my job seriously. Keeping the other guy safe is—"

Greg held a hand up to stop him. He looked embarrassed. "I know, I know. I'm sorry. You're one of the safest guys in the ring, which was why I was so surprised when Dillon told me you injured him. What happened? Dillon said it was like you were on another planet."

AJ looked back and checked that the others were out of earshot. Not that they would understand a conversation about the art of wrestling. Only Greg knew the business – because he helped rehab most of the guys when they picked up injuries, not because he had any love for it. In fact, it was astounding how little Greg knew about the history of pro wrestling. His knowledge began and ended with Hulk Hogan – the yellow pants version.

AJ put his hands on his hips and sighed. "I don't know what happened. I was bleeding from a cut, and it got in my eyes. My timing was off. I couldn't see."

Greg raised an eyebrow. "You couldn't see? Tractor must have really opened you up."

"It wasn't that bad a cut, but it was enough to disorientate me at the worst time."

"Okay, man, I'm sorry for bringing it up. You sure you don't want me to check out your shoulder?"

AJ put a hand on his injured joint and immediately felt a dull throb. "Maybe later. I'll see how it goes."

Greg peered up at the darkening sky. "You know, this is

like something from a horror movie. Are you trying to scare the shit out of the girls, or what? You picked the scariest goddamn place in the whole park. I keep expecting Jason to pop up and chop our heads off."

AJ laughed. "I promise, I'm not trying to scare you all. It's just a bit of fun."

"Yeah, well, let's find a way into this monstrosity, shall we?"

AJ stepped into the helmet's interior. A collection of pipework ran down from the ceiling and snaked back and forth on both sides. It must have been where the steam – part of the ride's atmospherics – had come from. There were also remnants of a light strip that likely formed the glowing red eyes inside the helmet.

Greg picked up a faded pamphlet from the ground. The front cover was a full-page advert for Frenzy. "They really went all out for this thing, huh? A shame, really. Nothing ever lasts."

AJ knelt and started pulling great handfuls of weeds away from the rear of the helmet. The tangles were blocking the entrance to the queuing area. "This would have been the way in. Help me clear a path for Ben."

Greg moved beside AJ and clawed at the weeds. It didn't take them long to remove the worst of it, but it still looked unwelcoming.

"How's it going in there?" Samantha called.

"It's going fine," said AJ. "Come in."

The rest of them moved cautiously into the helmet's dark interior. Ben started making ghost noises as he wheeled himself into the shadows.

"Stop it," said Tasha. "Don't mess around."

AJ shot Ben a look. The last thing they needed was Tasha

freaking out and refusing to go inside. "We've cleared a way to the queuing area. Come on."

"You sure it's safe?" Ashley put a hand out and leant against Greg so that she could lift her ankle away from the ground.

"So long as we're careful, it'll be fine."

"Okay then."

They headed through the rear of the helmet and found themselves in another overgrown area. Thick weeds had uprooted the paving slabs and formed a messy lawn. The only gap in the greenery was a patch of dark brown in the centre.

Greg placed the crook of his elbow over his nose and growled. "God sake, is this park where animals come to die?"

AJ inspected the carcass and wondered what it had been. Large grey feathers poked out among the gore. A large bird, maybe a goose. "They probably think it's safe," AJ offered. "They come in through the helmet and find this closed-off area. It's the type of place a sick animal would seek out to rest."

"Or die," said Ben.

AJ shrugged. "I suppose so."

"So this ride could be stuffed with a thousand animal corpses," said Ben. "You're going to owe me a new set of tyres."

AJ didn't want to give anyone time to freak out, so he moved past the sticky corpse and headed for the ride building. The original structure had been built to look like a cave, but it had been rethemed to resemble an old stone temple. Runic symbols dotted the various stony outcroppings, and an old man's face formed around the entrance. The doorway had been built to resemble the old man's mouth.

"Woden's temple," said AJ in awe. "It's even more

amazing than I thought it would be." While he knew the others would be less impressed than he was, they did stand there in silence and stare. It really did look like something centuries old, like Stonehenge or a Roman ruin.

"Can I just ask," said Ashley, "who is Woden?"

AJ looked at her and shrugged. "No idea. I think he's just a really old god from before, you know, *our* God came along."

"It's all bullshit to me," said Ben, "however old."

AJ wasn't religious either, but it was still interesting to think of how people once lived. "The entrance is right here." He pointed to the old man's stony mouth. "Should we try and force it open?"

Greg shrugged off his rucksack, rolled both his shoulders, then stepped forward. "Let me take a look."

The mouth would originally have been left open, but when the ride had been shut down, it had been boarded up. Greg was able to get his fingers into a gap between the boards, and he began pulling at it in a rowing motion. The muscles in his wide back bulged, and AJ had to marvel at his flared lats in appreciation. It took a lot of work to get a body like Greg's. Obsession even.

"Damn it!" Greg's jowls bulged as he strained. "It's nailed down tight. AJ, get in here next to me and help."

AJ threw off his rucksack and bent beside Greg. He forced his fingers through the narrow gap and pulled. He worried about hurting his hands, but gradually he increased his effort until he felt the boards begin to creak.

"It's coming," said Greg. "Keep pulling."

AJ gritted his teeth and placed his feet against the lowest boards, heaving with all his strength.

His entire body exploded with pain as he felt some part of him *pop*.

He fell onto his back, screaming.

"AJ!" Samantha ran to his aid. "What's wrong?"

"Ah! My shoulder!" He clutched his upper chest, wishing he could rip the pain right out. "Jesus, it hurts."

Greg was on him immediately, probing at him with his fingers. He pressed down hard with his palm and some of the pain went away. "Is that better?" AJ nodded, although it still hurt too much to want to talk. "Damn it, you should've come to me as soon as you knew you were hurt. I think you might have torn your rotator cuff. What are you playing at? This is your career."

"I-It's okay. I just tweaked it."

Greg swore. "You haven't tweaked it, you moron. Ashley, hand me my rucksack."

Like an obedient child, Ashley hurried to do as she was told. Greg rummaged through the pockets of his pack until he found a bottle of water and a foil packet. "Take a couple of these," he said, shoving pills into AJ's mouth and making him drink from the bottle. "They won't fix the damage, but they'll numb the pain."

AJ struggled to get the pills down his throat while lying on his back and he felt them stick in his oesophagus. "W-What are they?"

"Painkillers. Strong ones. You need to lie still and let them do their job."

"W-We need to get inside the ride."

Greg nodded. "Let me handle that. The job's halfway done."

AJ frowned then turned his head. Before his shoulder had torn, the two of them had at least succeeded in getting one of the boards loose. It hung in place now by only a single long nail, ready to be plucked free. A gap big enough to crawl through.

Frenzy awaited them.

CHAPTER ELEVEN

It took about ten minutes for the pills to kick in, and AJ sighed with relief when a fuzziness washed over him. The pain was still there, but it was now a background event, bothering only the back of his mind.

Greg climbed inside the ride first while the rest of them waited and listened to the sounds of him rooting around. After a minute, he popped his head through the gap in the boards with a smile on his face. "I still think this whole thing is stupid, but I have to admit it's pretty cool in here. All looks safe. Come on in."

And so they entered through the gap one after another. Samantha had to help AJ, as his coordination was all over the place, and he more or less fell through the gap.

Greg got busy placing a bunch of LED lanterns around the new area. While this was the first time they'd gone urban exploring together, AJ and Greg had gone hiking many times before and had camped in the Beacons three or four times. Neither of them were amateurs at this, and Greg – being Greg – had to have the fanciest equipment.

The battery-powered lanterns lit the interior in a ghostly

white glow, turning the cave-like space into an otherworldly grotto. The stony walls glistened and shone as tiny granules of glass or some other material caught the light, and when AJ reached out to touch one of the surfaces, he discovered it was fake. Some kind of cement, not real stone.

Tasha yelped. Everyone turned to face her as she stumbled about in the semi-darkness. Her yelps then turned to curses as she placed a hand across her chest. "Goddamn thing scared the life out of me."

AJ studied the figure standing at the back of the room and chuckled. It was some sort of primitive shaman, or perhaps a druid – he wasn't sure on the difference. The elderly white-haired man was stooped over and leaning on a gnarled walking stick the length of his body. He wore an animal skin but no shoes. The flesh around his eyes was dark and baggy.

"He's so lifelike," said Ashley, prodding at the old man's spongey cheeks. Her ankle seemed a little better, and her limp was now a stiff hobble. "He even feels real."

"One of the ride's animatronics," said AJ. "They were unparalleled at the time."

"They're unparalleled now," said Ben. "Look at that thing. Shame it's switched off. I would've liked to have seen it in motion."

"It would've disappointed you," AJ told him. "While they got the realism just right, the robotics back then were pretty awful. I saw a YouTube video once, taken from somebody's camcorder. The animatronics were really jerky."

Tasha had her arms folded as if she was holding herself. "Well, if this thing moves an inch, I'm gonna have a heart attack."

"Should we make camp here?" asked Samantha.

AJ shook his head. "It would be better to put another

wall between us and that draught." He was referring to the broken board where they came in. Already he could feel a chill. "This is the pre-ride area. The next room should be the embarkation platform. It should be large enough to make a camp."

"Okey-dokey," said Ben. "Lead the way."

They all grabbed a lantern as AJ took them through a wooden doorway beside the creepy druid figure. It was a normal door, but it had been painted to look as though it was carved from thick, elderly wood. The hinges were clogged with debris, so it needed a good push to open, but eventually it gave way and allowed them through.

The next room was even more impressive than the last. It was a wider area, with a high, curved ceiling, and at the back were a pair of trains themed to look like ancient fishing boats. They sat on a track, which AJ knew had originally been submerged in water to make a pretend river.

"There's plenty of room here," said Samantha, then she scuffed her foot over the bare cement. "Ground's a bit hard though."

"The rest of the ride will be too cramped," said AJ, "and there'll be tracks running through it. This area is as good as it's going to get. Plus, it's not too scary, huh, Tasha?"

Tasha managed to unfold her arms and placed her hands on her hips. "I'm a wimp, I know, but I'm doing my best, okay?"

"She hasn't pissed herself in five minutes," said Ben, waving his lantern in his sister's face and irritating her.

Tasha kicked his tyre. "Let's just get set up so we can start drinking. I'm starving too."

"I'll get the beans on," said Greg.

Tasha looked at him. "Huh?"

Greg shrugged. "I brought a stove and some baked beans. Can't have a camp without some beans on the go."

"I'll stick to the sarnies and crisps I brought with me, thanks."

"Suit yourself."

AJ opened up his rucksack and pulled out some of his things. He had brought his iPad with him, fully charged, and he set it up with some portable speakers. A minute later they had nineties Britpop blaring and the entire atmosphere changed. Sleeping bags were dispensed. Snacks were opened. And booze flowed. AJ was already feeling light-headed, but he downed another beer with relish, enjoying the warm feeling it gave his legs. His shoulder throbbed constantly, and he struggled to move it, but overall he was feeling good. A little high and a little drunk, maybe, but not in a bad place at all.

AJ went and took a seat in one of the ride trains, grateful that the cushions were still intact. His fresh beer sat securely on the lap bar, which was convenient, so he placed both hands behind his head and leant back. "This might be my spot for the evening," he told the others.

Samantha climbed in next to him, sloshing white wine in a plastic cup. "How's your shoulder?"

"Probably ruined, but those pills Greg gave me were pretty hardcore."

"Will it screw everything up for you?"

He frowned at her. "What do you mean?"

"Your contract to go wrestle in the States… Will they still take you with an injury?"

"Oh, um, yeah, I'm sure it'll be fine. I just need to rest and let myself heal. You know Greg, he likes to look on the negative side of life. It's not that bad, really. I get hurt all the time. Part of the job."

"I'm really proud of you. This has always been your dream. Even when people made fun of you at school, you kept at it with your head held high. No one will be laughing when you're making millions."

"I'm a long way from that. Wrestling is a tough living, even at the top. If I was in it for the money, I would've quit a long time ago."

"So why *do* you love it so much?"

He shrugged. "I was stuck at home a lot as a kid, looking after mum. You know how it was for me back then."

She nodded. It had always caused issues when they had first become friends. Everyone would make plans together, but AJ could hardly ever make them. Even going down the park had been too much of a commitment for him.

He shrugged again. "I watched a lot of television, and wrestling on a Friday night was my escape. My real life was so dull, but these big, colourful characters on TV were always having fun and causing mayhem. I was a powerless little kid trapped in the house, looking after a blind woman, but Stone Cold was out raising hell while The Rock was humiliating anyone who dared face him. I needed to know that life could be unpredictable instead of an endless existence of routine and chores."

Samantha gave him a thin-lipped smile. "That makes sense. It must have been fun to live in a world full of heroes and villains constantly doing battle."

AJ smiled back at her. "I see the way little kids in the audience look at me when I wrestle, and I know I'm giving them that same gift, showing them that they can put themselves on display and be who they want to be one day. That the powerlessness of childhood doesn't last forever. Kids need to know the future is whatever they want to make it."

Samantha chuckled, but she wasn't mocking him. The

way she looked at him was all compassion, and possibly something more. "Wow. I thought people watched wrestling for the violence."

AJ took a swig from his beer. "They do, and I allow them to experience it without anyone getting hurt."

She raised an eyebrow at him. "From the way you were screaming in pain earlier, I don't think that's true. You be careful in the States, okay? I know you – you'll give a hundred and ten to impress everyone, but it's not worth it if you end up broken."

"Yeah, well, that's all in the future. Tell me how things are with you. I never see you any more."

She looked down into her cup and swirled the wine around as if it were a magical whirlpool that would show her whatever she wanted. He was sure her hair was shorter, and for the first time, he saw slight wrinkles at the corners of her eyes. "Yeah, well, working for myself isn't all it's cracked up to be."

"Really? I thought you were doing great."

"I am, so long as I work every hour God sends. There's so much competition out there. I trained to be an accountant because I thought I would be able to work for myself and make a good living, but it seems like everyone else had the same idea. If I lower my prices any more, I'll be on minimum wage. If I increase them, my customers will go elsewhere. And people expect so much for their money. Some of my clients give me a carrier bag full of receipts and expect me to make sense of it within a week. It's horrible. Worst decision I ever made."

"So quit."

"And then what? Go work for someone else? You were at Alscon with me. Don't you remember how John used to be? Trying to get me into bed every time I made the mistake of smiling at him? Having a boss is just as much a nightmare. Life just seems shit whatever I decide to do. That's why I'm so happy for *you*. At least someone has a bright future to look forward to. I just wish it wasn't going to take you so far away."

He shook his head and gave a sad smile. "I've only been on the other side of town, and this is the first time I've seen you in months."

"I kept thinking things would get better. That all the hard work up front would pay off down the line. I'm still waiting for that to happen. I miss you too. I've been thinking about you a lot lately. Maybe I took for granted how much you meant to me. Hey, perhaps you can take me to the States with you. I can be your accountant-slash-mistress."

AJ felt a butterfly take flight in his tummy. "My mistress, ay? Didn't know you thought about me like that."

She shrugged one shoulder. "Have you seen *you?* A girl can do a lot worse. And now you're going to be rich and famous too."

"Again, a long way from that. But nice to know you don't objectify me in any way." He gave her a playful nudge and then flipped his long blonde hair. "Anyway, I don't want to think about it tonight."

She tilted her head at him. "Why not?"

"Because it'll make me sad that I'm not going to be able to hang out with you all any more. I just want to enjoy being with my friends one last time before everything changes."

"You're right, that is depressing." She took a swig of wine and placed a hand on his leg. The warmth from her palm spread throughout his thigh and he hoped she left it there. It was weird. Nothing had ever happened between them – their friendship had always been too important, too *ingrained* – but perhaps drifting apart had changed things, made their friendship less of an obstacle.

Or was he just tipsy from the drugs and alcohol?

But she was the one who put her hand on my knee.

She's my favourite person. Always has been. I'll miss her the most. I'll miss looking at her like this.

AJ put his hand on top of hers, seeing how it felt. It felt right. Then he smiled at her. "You want to go exploring? Check this place out properly?"

Her eyes flicked away. Either he had got the wrong impression and made her feel awkward, or she was nervous about exploring Frenzy's belly. If he was honest, he was nervous too, but that's what made it so much fun.

"Yeah, I'm up for exploring a bit. Will it, um, be safe? I mean, this part of the ride was meant for people, but you're talking about, what, walking along the tracks?"

"There's no power, so nothing dangerous can happen. Going from the state of the first two rooms, I think the rest of the ride will be in good shape too. A catwalk should run alongside the track all the way round, so we just need to stay on it. We'll be fine."

She smiled. "Then let's go for a walk."

He offered her his hand and stood up. "A gentleman would be most honoured to escort a lady."

"Such manners. A man may receive a lady's handkerchief."

Both chuckling, they climbed out of the fishing boat and headed for the open archway devouring the tracks ahead. It was meant to resemble the mouth of a cave, but in the subdued light, it just looked like a deep black hole.

AJ grabbed one of Greg's LED lanterns. "I need to take one of these, Greg. That cool?"

Greg had already started heating up some beans in a

mess tin over his portable stove. Ben and Tasha were sitting with him while Ashley was waving her phone about in the corner. "Where you two off to?" he asked in a tone that seemed oddly disapproving.

"I just want to check out the ride," said AJ, shrugging.

"You can come if you want?" said Samantha, which confused AJ once again as to what she was thinking. Was she scared to be alone with him? Or just acting normally?

Stop overthinking things, AJ.

Greg looked at AJ with a strange expression, and if AJ didn't know better, he would've said he could see a glimmer of hurt in his friend's eyes. Did Greg have a thing for Samantha? That would be crazy – AJ didn't even know if *he* had a thing for Samantha – because Greg was with Ashley.

"That cool, man?" AJ asked again.

The strange expression dropped from Greg's face, and he shrugged the boulders that counted for his shoulders. "Yeah, whatever, man. I'll catch you up in a bit, unless I'd be interrupting something?"

AJ huffed. "Why are you being weird?"

"I'm not. I just thought we'd explore this place together."

Ben tutted. "You need a cuddle or something, man? No one's leaving you out, Greg. We're gonna be partying all night, so let the lovebirds go for their walk."

"We're not lovebirds," said Samantha, clearly embarrassed by the suggestion. "We're just going to take a look around."

"Yeah," said AJ, realising now how stupid he was for thinking anything would happen between them. They were just friends. "I've been looking forward to checking this place out for a year. I'm just a bit eager."

Greg turned his attention to his sizzling beans. "Yeah, no problem. Go have fun. Like I said, I'll catch up."

AJ gave Samantha a little nudge, letting her know he was ready to exit this strange conversation. She looked at him and nodded, then whispered, "That was weird. Now I want to go exploring in the dark even more just to get away from this atmosphere. Shall we depart?"

"Yes, my lady. Let's do so at once."

They headed through the archway and into the tunnel. Into darkness.

CHAPTER TWELVE

The LED lantern cast silver shadows over everything and gave the tunnel an almost heavenly aura. Samantha edged along the catwalk, her wine sloshing in its cup. "I can't believe we're doing this. How much trouble would we be in if we got caught here?"

"Probably none," said AJ. "Technically, we're trespassing, but it's not like we're stealing or intending to bury a body. It's just a bit of mischief."

"The night is still young. Who knows what could happen."

He smirked at her in the gloom. "You plan on killing someone?"

"Why d'you think I agreed to come this weekend? I've been planning on murdering you all for years. Starting with you!" She pretended to stab him, poking him in the ribs and making him snigger. He grabbed her wrists and fought her away playfully.

"Always thought you might be a serial killer," he said, still holding her arms. "You have that look about you."

"If I killed you all tonight, wouldn't that make me a spree

killer? To be a serial killer, I would have to space the murders out, right?"

"It's scary that you know that."

"Netflix teaches one a lot about murdering."

AJ smirked. "God bless streaming services, the saviour of the antisocial. I can't tell you the amount of times I've watched *Fawlty Towers* at three in the morning."

Samantha was about to reply, but she unexpectedly stumbled. AJ grabbed her waist and kept her from falling off the narrow catwalk. She ended up laughing hysterically as he held her in his arms.

"Yikes, are you okay?" he asked her.

"Yeah, I *am* okay. I'm having a nice time. God, it feels good just to take a break and act stupid for a night." She sipped her wine, which she had somehow managed not to spill. "I think I'm a bit tipsy."

"Me too," AJ admitted, and it felt good. It wasn't just Samantha who needed a break. He'd been under a lot of stress himself. A lot on his mind. For tonight, at least, he could let it all go.

Samantha made no attempt to remove herself from his grasp, so the two of them just stood there embracing. The longer it went on, the less AJ wanted it to end.

I'm not imagining this, right?

Eventually, Samantha broke away. She stared down the tunnel ahead and lifted AJ's arm so that he held the lantern a little higher. Light spilled further along the tracks. "Hey, AJ, what's that?"

They walked along the catwalk and reached a wider area. A village scene featuring a family of four emaciated figures – a man and a woman huddled together with their starving children. They were all staring up at the sky as if in prayer.

AJ cast light over each of the faces and shuddered at how real their desperation appeared.

Samantha pulled a face and pressed close against him. "That's disturbing."

"It's just part of the ride's narrative," he said, more to himself than to her. "Guests play the part of fishermen during a famine. It's up to us to feed the village, but we have to make a pact with Woden first. A sacrifice must be made."

"A sacrifice?"

He nodded. "The ride's big finale. I'll let you find out what it is for yourself."

She groaned. "Oh, it's not going to scare me, is it?"

He just smiled. They walked on past the village scene and continued on to the next area. Originally, the little fishing boats would have passed through an area of swampland with dead fish – just props, of course – floating on the water. But now the pretend river was dry, and the tracks, along with their sudden bumps and shuffles, were exposed.

As AJ cast the glow of his lantern, he discovered several nozzles embedded into the fake scenery. They were part of the ride's atmospherics, intended to spray water and gusts of air. The overall effect must have been fantastic. He wished he could have ridden Frenzy in its prime.

"Stinks in here." Samantha put the back of one hand against her nose.

AJ saw mould all over the tracks. "There was probably standing water here for years," he said. "This area was meant to be a foul swamp and, ironically, it probably became one after they abandoned it. Come on, let's check out a bit more before we rejoin the others."

Samantha swigged the last of her wine. "Yeah, I need a top-up before I murder you all."

The next part of the ride was when the thrills would have started in earnest. The track dropped suddenly and turned a sharp right into a new area unseen from the swamp. It was a wide trench that would also once have been full of water. A couple of machines stood mounted on either side of the tracks and would have created waves. The most impressive part of the scene was the gigantic face glaring down at them from above.

Samantha stopped on the catwalk and stared up at the huge face in awe. "I take it this is Woden?"

"Yeah, I think this where people on the boat would've made a deal with Woden to end the famine. The original ride had audio. Woden spoke in this horrible booming voice. His whole face moved. The boat would have rocked about too, almost capsizing. It must have been terrifying."

"It's terrifying *now*, even without all of that. That thing is huge. It's like the faces on the mountain in America. Mount Rushmore, right?"

AJ nodded. "It's certainly something. I don't know how the ride makers managed it. Even Disney would have struggled to create something like this back then. Maybe even now."

The face wasn't flesh, but a mixture of stone and wood – like a mountain and an oak tree had birthed a monstrous child. The eyes were jet-black glass and the scowling lips were like two oak branches pressed together. Hair dangled from the massive head in straggly, snake-like vines.

"The eyes used to light up red," said AJ. "The lips moved, the hair dangled. Wow."

Samantha was grinning at him. "You're so cute. Next month, we're going to Alton Towers, okay? I need a day off, and I want to spend it with you acting like an excited kid."

"You think I'm an excited kid?"

She rubbed his arm, awakening the pain in his shoulder "It's a good thing. It's infectious."

Despite the pain, AJ didn't move away. Samantha looked into his eyes. She began to lean forward.

"We should, um, head back," said AJ, suddenly feeling weak in the legs. For some reason he was panicking. He tried to tell himself that he was just being mindful of Greg. It was right that they should discover at least part of the ride together as a group. They should go back and get him.

Samantha frowned at him. "Oh, yeah, okay. You're right. We came here to be together."

AJ nodded and smiled, but he felt like he was smiling awkwardly. His lips felt stretched out and flat. He was suddenly very self-aware. "M-Maybe we can talk some more later."

"Yeah, sure. You're just thinking about Greg and his beans, aren't you?"

"Ha! You know me so well."

They turned around and headed back along the catwalk. The stench of the swamp hit them before they got there, and AJ felt the back of his neck tingle as he walked away from the giant stone face glaring at their back. He had the strange feeling that it might suddenly come alive while he wasn't looking, bright red eyes flashing with hatred. But when he glanced back, the face hadn't moved. Silent. Still. Implacable.

Something rushed across the tracks in front of them and made both of them yelp. The shadow raced in and out of the lantern's narrow glow. Samantha hopped back and almost fell off the catwalk again.

AJ caught her once more, his shoulder grumbling at the act. "It's just a rat."

"Oh, it's just a rat, is it? No problem. Just a dirty, bitey little rat. With rabies."

"What do you expect? Animals make their homes where people aren't."

"Well, now people *are*, so they need to bugger off."

AJ grinned. "I'll send out a memo. Come on, they won't bother us if we don't bother them."

Samantha walked hurriedly. As much as she was a modern, confident woman, she still wet herself at the sight of spiders and mice.

They made it back to the village scene and were faced once again with those starving children and their desperate parents. AJ tried to angle the lantern so as not to highlight their emaciated faces, but he quickly realised something was wrong.

The father figure was missing.

AJ grabbed Samantha's wrist, accidentally hurting her. "I'm sorry," he said, "just... one of the figures has disappeared."

She frowned. "What are you...? Oh my God. Oh my God! Are you messing around? The dad is missing! Where did he go?"

AJ studied the tunnel ahead, but all he saw was shadows and the gentle glint of the tracks. No way could the figure have moved on its own. It was an animatronic, and there wasn't any power.

So where was it? Where was the emaciated, starving father?

AJ moved in front of Samantha, keeping a hand on her so he knew she was there. "Stay still. Let's just... We shouldn't panic."

"Too late. Already there. You said they're animatronics, right? So how could it have moved without any electricity?"

AJ squeezed her arm. "I don't know. Let me think for a second."

Something shifted in the darkness again, moved across the tracks in a zigzag. Another rat maybe?

Please let it be a rat.

Something moved again, this time closer.

With a scream, Samantha shoved past AJ and made a run for it.

"Sam! Wait!"

She didn't turn back. Fear had taken her reins.

"Goddammit, Sam, stop!"

AJ took off after her, knowing he would probably slip off the catwalk and break an ankle. Terror jolted through his bones, but his mind couldn't rationalise. What was he afraid of? That a lifeless chunk of steel and plastic had somehow come alive? It was ridiculous. There would be a simple explanation.

He would laugh at himself any moment now.

Please let me laugh at myself.

Come on, just show me the punchline.

The lantern bounced as AJ ran, light spiralling across the floor, the walls, the ceiling. Samantha's silhouette raced frantically ahead – she was barely looking where she was going.

AJ tried to catch up with her. He was faster, no question, but he was hurt. He gritted his teeth and picked up as much speed as he could. His boot came down on the edge of the catwalk, more off than on. His leg folded and he fell onto the steel track. His ribs broke his landing and all his breath escaped him in an anguished howl.

"AJ!" Samantha stopped running and turned back towards him. "AJ, where are you?"

AJ couldn't speak. He was winded. A strangled moan escaped him, but that was all.

"AJ, hold on, I-I'm coming back."

He tried to sit up, to wave her off so that she could get Greg and the others, but she continued racing back towards him.

And so did something else.

A silhouette stalked Samantha, moving mechanically right behind her. Moving *jerkily*. Samantha had no idea she was being followed. Preyed upon.

AJ fought to catch his breath. "S-S-Sam!"

"I see you! I'm right here."

"N-No! Turn... turn... around!"

Samantha didn't seem to understand him. She'd spotted him lying on the tracks and was hurrying along the catwalk towards him. "AJ, what happened?"

The silhouette moved past her shoulder.

"B-Behind you!"

Samantha frowned in the light of the lantern, which he had somehow managed to hold on to. Finally, it dawned on her that AJ was trying to warn her.

Her expression froze. She started to turn around.

A figure leapt out of the shadows.

The emaciated father glared at them. The animatronic's cold, dead eyes caught the light and shone white. Somehow, it was alive.

Samantha screamed, stumbled, and fell right on top of AJ. The two of them cowered on the tracks.

The emaciated father stopped at the edge of the catwalk, glaring down at them.

AJ clutched Samantha tightly against himself, both of them trembling. What the hell was going on?

Laughter echoed in the tunnel and Greg's face appeared from behind the emaciated father, beaming so wide that his teeth caught the glow of the LED lantern. "Guys, I'm so sorry. It was just supposed to be a prank. Are you both okay? Jesus, you two are a pair of clowns."

AJ was furious, but he was also so relieved that he was unable to do anything but lie there and pant. His heart was still in his throat. Samantha, on the other hand, didn't have that problem. "Greg? You fucking arsehole! What the hell are you playing at?"

Greg's grin faded a little as he realised his joke had gone too far. "I'm sorry. I was just mucking about. Seriously, are you both okay?"

Samantha climbed off AJ and pulled herself back up onto the catwalk. She approached Greg with such ferocity that Greg, twice her size, backed off. She poked him right in the centre of his bulky chest. "No, we are *not* fucking okay. AJ's hurt."

"I'm okay," said AJ, rubbing his ribs. He was pretty sure they weren't broken. He'd managed to catch his breath and most of the pain was gone. His shoulder was slowly throbbing back to life though. "Just help me up out of this ditch."

"Sure thing." Greg hopped down into the trench and helped peel AJ off the tracks. The fall had only been a few feet, but the steel tracks didn't make a soft place to land.

"I could have really been hurt," said AJ. "You're lucky I fall on my back for a living."

Greg helped him onto the catwalk and nodded earnestly. "You're right, I'm sorry. My aim was only to scare you. I didn't know you'd fall."

"I shouldn't have run off," said Samantha, cooling down now that she had expelled her anger. "Sorry. I overreacted."

AJ shrugged. "It's okay. It was pretty terrifying."

"You see?" said Greg, beaming. "It was awesome, admit it. I totally got you both."

"No," said Samantha. "You're an arsehole."

Greg turned and picked up the emaciated father figure and started walking it forward, shuffling it along like a kid playing with a toy. "I came looking for you and I couldn't resist it. The characters in this place are better than Tussaud's. If you didn't know better, you'd say this was a real starving human being, right? Look at this guy. His eyes are bloodshot, his teeth are dirty. I can almost imagine the smell of his ball sweat."

AJ rubbed at his ribs. "Yeah, it's great. Let's get out of the dark. I need another drink. Maybe some more of your painkillers too."

Greg frowned. "Pace yourself, mate. The night's only just started."

"Yeah," said Samantha, punching Greg in the back. "And you nearly ended it. No more jokes, you hear me?"

Greg rolled his eyes. "Okay, okay, no more messing around, I promise. No more surprises."

You better hope so, thought AJ, more in pain with every step. *Because I won't let you ruin this weekend for me.*

CHAPTER THIRTEEN

"I TAKE it Greg's plan to sneak up and scare the life out of you worked?" said Ashley as they clambered back up onto the embarkation platform. She was sitting down now with her phone stowed away, which meant she had failed to find a signal. The device would still be in her hand otherwise. Instead, she now had her expensive camera out of its bag and perched across her knees while she sat around Greg's portable campfire. She also had a half-finished bottle of wine next to her bare, swollen ankle. The LED lanterns had been spaced evenly, lighting up most of the platform now.

"We heard you screaming," said Ben. "I assumed someone had been killed."

Samantha side-eyed Greg. "It was close. It's dangerous back there on the tracks."

"Could have gone bad." AJ rubbed his ribs.

Ashley scowled at Greg. "I told you not to do it, you idiot. Why did you want to interrupt them, anyway?"

"I wasn't interrupting them. They were just chatting. Get off my back, Ash."

She lifted her camera and took a quick snap of his face. "There's another one for the grumpy books."

Tasha sat on the floor nearby, eating a sandwich. She spoke with her mouth half-full. "We saw a rat while you were gone. Ran right across the floor and into the first room."

Samantha shuddered. "Yeah, we saw one too. This whole place is probably infested."

"They're just scrounging," said Greg. "Long as we keep our rubbish in the next room they won't bother us in here."

"Unless they eat my foot while I'm sleeping," said Ben. "I wouldn't feel it. I'd just wake up in the morning with bloody stumps."

Tasha pulled the sandwich away from her mouth and groaned. "Bloody hell, Ben, d'you have to? I'm eating."

"I don't like being around all these rats," said Ashley.

"Stop freaking out," Greg told her. "Rats are scavengers, not lions. Just ignore them and they'll ignore you."

"They carry disease."

"That's city rats."

"How d'you know?"

Greg shrugged. "Because I know everything. Now, just shut up and talk about something else."

Ashley took another snapshot of his face. "Dick!"

"What is with you two?" Ben was shaking his head. "You're like an old married couple." There was chill in the air as Greg and Ashley shot each other a look. Ben caught the exchange and frowned. "What? What did I say?"

Ashley stood with her camera and walked away. "Nothing," she said. "Let's just enjoy ourselves. It'll make a change." She started snapping pictures of the fishing boats and various other parts of the scenery. Samantha went after her, eventually striking a sexy pose in front of one of the boats as the two girls conducted an impromptu photoshoot.

AJ went and sat with the others while Greg paced alone. It was several moments before he decided to sit down as well. He inserted himself between Tasha and Ben.

"You okay, mate?" Ben asked as he handed Greg a beer. "You don't seem right."

"I'm fine. Me and Ash have just been fighting a lot lately, that's all."

"What about?" asked Tasha, displaying no tact at all. She wasn't a subtle person by any means.

Greg rotated the beer bottle in his hand, studying the label. Then he turned to watch Ashley for a moment over by the boats. "We've been arguing about marriage. That's what you said wrong, Ben. You said the M word. Ash wants to tie the knot, but I... I just don't think it's for me. Not yet."

Tasha took a bite of her sandwich and spoke with her mouth full again. "Aren't you, like, thirty?"

Greg scowled. "I'm twenty-eight."

"Big diff! I'm pretty sure Ashley is being reasonable by wanting to get married before she's thirty. Why don't you want to? You've been together a while, haven't you?"

"Yeah, but who knows how long we'll make it. Maybe forever. Maybe not."

"You're a fool," said Ben, "if you're waiting for someone better to come along. Ashley's a diamond."

Greg nodded, and he seemed to realise he didn't have the crowd on his side. "Yeah, of course, I agree. Suppose I just didn't realise I'd got to this point, you know? Being married, having kids, all that. Always seemed a long way off, you know?"

AJ cracked open a beer and swigged from it, then gasped and wiped his lips. "Still seems that way for me. If you have someone who loves you and wants to be with you, you're lucky. Don't take it for granted."

Greg nodded and held a hand up. "Okay, okay, give me a break. Ash and I will work through it. Relationships have their ups and downs, that's all. You'd know that if you weren't all a bunch of pathetic singletons."

AJ ignored the insult and patted his friend on his broad back. It was like slapping granite. "I'd just love to see you two settled and happy. You'd both owe me for the rest of your lives for hooking you up."

"I'll buy you an Amazon gift card and we'll call it even." Greg raised an eyebrow at Ben. "So what's new with you, man? Ain't seen you in a while."

"I've been working a lot. I got office manager a couple of months back. Decent money, but boring as hell."

"Congratulations," said Greg. "You always were the sensible one."

"Cheers."

"He's joined a choir as well," said Tasha with a smirk.

AJ leant forward. "He did *what*?"

Ben gave Tasha a deadly look, but it only lengthened the smirk on her face. "You had to tell them, didn't you?" He looked back at the others and began to blush. "It's not a choir, it's an amateur dramatics group. We put on shows at the local theatre. I'm new, so I don't have any on-stage parts, but I'm part of the choir."

"So you go up on stage..." Greg stopped mid-sentence to cover his mouth to keep from laughing. "Ahem, so you go up on stage and sing your little cotton socks off?"

Ben couldn't look him in the eye. "It's just a bit of fun, man. I enjoy singing. Always have. And it's a nice group of people. Sue me for having a hobby that doesn't involve lifting weight."

Greg was beaming like a flashlight. "Will you sing us a little number now? Please?"

"Screw you, man. Anyway, how is getting up on stage and performing *Peter Pan* any different to what AJ does? It's all just a show."

Greg clutched his chest. "You're doing *Peter Pan*? Please tell me if you get the part of Tinkerbell."

Ben looked at AJ and shook his head in disbelief. "My life is a joke to this guy. Haven't heard him laugh like this the whole time I've known him."

AJ chuckled. "He doesn't get out of the gym a lot. If it doesn't involve testosterone, he doesn't understand it."

Greg elbowed AJ. "Hey, man, I'm not just some muscle head. I read. I go to the theatre. Well, I went once. There were puppets."

Ben rolled his eyes. "Yeah, that was *Avenue Q*. It was nine months ago, man. I see it really made an impression."

Greg shrugged. "It was stupid. Like an episode of *South Park* but ninety minutes long and with a lot more singing. Hey, maybe you can get a gig with those guys? The puppet people."

"That would be sweet," said Ben. "I wouldn't have to see your ugly mug again for one thing."

Greg swigged his beer and belched. "You'd miss me, admit it!"

"Like a haemorrhoid on my arse."

AJ spat beer through his nose.

Samantha and Ashley returned to join them, finished with their photoshoot and attracted by the laughter. "What's so funny?" asked Ashley, sitting down next to Greg and putting her arm around him. Apparently she had got over her strop.

"Just guys being guys," Tasha explained. "Talking about their arses."

Samantha rolled her eyes and dropped down next to AJ. "Sounds about right. Who's got the wine?"

Tasha handed over the bottle she was working on and Samantha took it and filled her cup.

"Doesn't quite taste the same out of a plastic beaker, does it?" said Ashley, grabbing a fresh bottle and filling her own.

"Long as the end result is the same," said Samantha. She necked half the cup in one and then filled it back to the top.

"Maybe you should go easy," said Ben. "You'll be legless."

She rolled her eyes at him. "I'm just relaxing. Having fun" – she glared at Greg – "now that my heart rate has gone back to normal."

Greg raised his beer and grinned. "So how deep did you two get? I could hear your voices, but you sounded far away. Underground."

"We went down into this chamber," said Samantha. "It was pretty cool. There was a giant head."

Greg smirked. "A giant head?"

"Yeah, a giant head. You'll have to see for yourself, but it was impressive."

Ashley filled her cup, having already finished the wine she'd just poured. "When are we going to take the tour? I wanna see the head."

Greg grabbed his crotch. "If it's head you're interested in."

Everyone groaned.

Ashley rolled her eyes. "He says that, but if I dared try to touch it, he'd make an excuse."

Anger flashed across Greg's face, and he shrugged her arm off him. "Will you shut the fuck up? No one wants to hear about our love life."

"What love life? You haven't touched me in months."

"Oh, don't exaggerate."

Ashley showed her teeth, and with her wild red hair she resembled a feral woodland creature. "My sister's birthday."

"What?"

"My sister's birthday. That was the last time we fucked. And only then because you were drunk. My sister's birthday is January fifteenth. Two months ago, Greg."

He looked at the others, then chuckled with embarrassment. "W-We've done it since then. She's just being dramatic. Too much to drink."

Ben shrugged. "Hey, it makes no odds to me, man. I don't need to know your dick's schedule."

"Sounds like it doesn't have one," said Tasha, covering a smirk with her hand.

Ashley broke out in cackles.

It was the final straw.

Greg shot up off the floor and kicked the half-empty wine bottle next to Ashley. It hurtled through the air and struck the side of one of the fishing boats. Miraculously, it didn't smash. It just *clonked* and rolled across the floor, oozing a trail of wine.

AJ leapt up, startled by the sudden outburst. "Whoa, mate. Calm down."

Greg ignored AJ and pointed his finger in Ashley's face. Ashley continued smirking, which didn't help matters. "I am so sick of your bullshit, Ash. All you do is nag me. Then you fucking moan that I don't want to marry you. Is there really any fucking surprise?"

"Oh, go wank off, you sad fuck."

AJ had never seen Greg make a face like the one he was making now, and he feared his friend might go off like a firework. He reached out and placed a hand on Greg's chest, easing him back gently. While AJ was no coward, if it came to blows, he wasn't sure he could handle his much bigger friend. He was like a barrel full of iron. "Come on, mate, take a breather, yeah?"

Greg was glaring at Ashley, and it seemed to take an effort for him to look away. "You're tearing me apart, Ashley."

AJ moved him away another step. "Just go into the other room. I'll grab some beers and we'll talk, okay? We're all a bit tipsy, but everything is fine."

Ashley went to say something, but Samantha shushed her. AJ was glad there was someone else trying to calm things down. What on earth was going on with Greg and Ashley? They were acting like they hated each other.

Greg stormed off, heading from the light of the lanterns and into the darkness of the first room they'd entered.

"Good riddance," said Ashley.

AJ stared at her, one of his oldest friends, and actually had an urge to slap her. "What is wrong with you, Ash? You're acting like a right cow."

Ashley recoiled. He never spoke to her like this, and it obviously upset her. Good. He didn't like her very much right now. He buried his disgust and went to help Greg. The guy might be an arsehole at the best of times, but he didn't deserve to be mocked like this. Before he took a lantern and left, he turned back to the others. "Have something to eat, you lot. Soak up some of that alcohol."

AJ found Greg inside the next room, kneeling beside the gap they had made between the boards. AJ left the lantern in the centre of the room and hurried over to interrupt whatever his friend was doing. "Hey, man, you okay?"

"I'm heading out. I don't care how long it takes me to find the road, but I'm leaving."

"Are you insane?" AJ checked his watch. "It's ten at night.

It'll be midnight by the time you reach the road, and then what? You're going to, what, get a taxi to take you sixty miles home? It'll cost an arm and a leg."

Greg stood and faced him. "Better than spending the night with that bitch."

"That's your girlfriend, man. You and Ash love each other. She's just a bit pissed."

"Yeah, tell me about it. I wish I could say it was a one-off."

"What d'you mean?"

"I mean she gets like this at least once a week and I'm sick of it. All she ever does is give me shit."

AJ needed to take a moment. He had never expected things to go this way. These were his friends. This was supposed to be a great time they would all remember. It was all going wrong. "Look, man, is something going on with you two? What is it with all the little digs she keeps making? Or how cold you're being with her?"

Greg seemed to shrivel with embarrassment. He tried to shrug it off but he couldn't. "We've lost a bit of our spark in the bedroom, that's all. What's the big deal? Things fade." He sighed as though he was unbearably tired. "Maybe Ashley has a high sex drive, or something, and I can't keep up with her."

AJ nodded, but he didn't know what to think. "Okay, well, can't you two just make up? There's no reason to fall out after a few harsh words."

Greg turned and kicked at the boards. An icy breeze whipped through the gap and harried AJ's ankles. Strange, because it had felt mild outside before they'd entered.

"Just calm down. What's got into you?"

"I just... I don't think I'm in love with Ashley any more."

He turned back to face AJ. "I just don't—" He stopped mid-sentence and looked past AJ.

AJ turned to see what Greg was looking at and saw Ashley standing there, holding a lantern. The harsh white glow made her look like a ghoul, and the haunted look in her eyes made it even more so. She shook her head in disbelief. "I... I came to apologise."

Greg groaned. "Ash, just wait a second, okay?"

Ashley turned and fled back into the other room. AJ started after them but stopped in his tracks. The hairs on the back of his neck stood up.

Something was wrong.

Not with Ashley or Greg. Something was wrong with the room. AJ picked up the lantern he had left in the centre of the room and raised it up to shoulder height. He crept towards the doorway, moving his eyes in every direction until his brain finally figured out what was amiss.

Then the answer came to him.

The druid statue had gone.

The creepy old man was missing. He hoped it was another one of Greg's jokes.

CHAPTER FOURTEEN

AJ HEARD SCREAMING, but it wasn't enough to make him move. He was transfixed on the spot where he was sure – positive – that the animatronic druid had stood. They had all seen it. Ashley had touched its face.

He's so lifelike.

But now it was gone.

The screaming in the next room continued as Greg and Ashley no doubt went at one another. Breaking up even. AJ couldn't believe it. His friends. But Greg and Ashley's relationship problems were not his chief concern right now.

What had happened to the druid?

Was it another of Greg's pranks? Where had he taken it? And when?

The screaming continued. It had been going on too long now to ignore. His mind conjured images of Greg beating on Ashley, or Ashley raking Greg's eyes. It was too much to bear.

AJ finally got moving. He stepped back into the other room and saw the others gathered around the campfire. It wasn't Greg and Ashley screaming at one another, but everyone screaming together and at once.

AJ hurried to Samantha's side and shook her. "What is it?"

She glanced at him but didn't seem to see him. Her eyes were open wide and staring right past him. Eventually, she was able to nod in the direction of the fishing boats. *Look.*

AJ turned. The light from the lanterns only just reached the fishing boats, which was why his eyes detected only shapes and shadows at first. Nothing easily, immediately identifiable. Just movement. It took him a while to realise he was watching rats scurrying. Hundreds of them. The rodents lined up along the edge of the platform, almost like they were queuing to go on the ride. Except they were facing the wrong way. They were facing AJ and the others. The light reflected off their beady black eyes like a night full of stars.

"W-What do they want?" Ashley managed to ask. She clutched her heavy camera as though it were a shield.

It was Ben who answered. "Th-They're rats. The only thing they care about is eating and shagging."

"They ain't doing either one to me," said Greg.

The rats didn't move. They just perched on their back feet, watching like sentries. Would they attack? If they did, there was enough of them to create a swarm. AJ's mind whirled, trying to answer the question of whether or not people had ever been eaten alive by rats. His rational mind kept shouting *no*. Another part of him whispered more horrifying answers.

"Everyone, back up slowly," said Greg. "I think we're being told to leave. This is clearly their turf."

They began to shuffle for the exit, but a sudden *clunk* made them stop.

"Guys, I'm stuck!" The small front wheel of Ben's chair

had wedged against the wine bottle Greg had kicked across the floor.

"Hold on, let me help." Carefully, AJ knelt and removed the bottle.

"Thanks. Been a really nice weekend, man. We'll have to do this again."

AJ nodded, not knowing what else to do. The rats were still standing in a line. They could have been puppets if not for their beady, reflective eyes.

"This is so fucked up," AJ muttered.

"Just keep moving," said Greg.

They shuffled along in a group, backing up towards the doorway. AJ's mind was still on the missing druid, but he told himself that Greg must have messed with it. No other explanation.

Maybe the goddamn horde of rats moved him.

Samantha passed through the doorway first, with Tasha right behind her, but before Tasha could follow, the rats burst into a chorus, a cacophonous screeching coming from every tiny snout. A bloodcurdling sound.

Tasha stopped and covered her ears. "What are they doing?"

The rats screeched louder.

"I don't know," said Ben. "Just get the hell out of here, sis."

Tasha went to make a move.

The rats shattered. That's how AJ would have described it. One second, they were bunched up in an orderly line, the next they were *shattering* in every direction. Their screeching continued, urgent and panicked now. Were they afraid?

If so, of what?

Samantha shouted from the other room. "Tasha! Come on."

Tasha nodded and snapped free of her shock. "Okay, I'm coming, I'm come—"

Thorny vines whipped out of nowhere and snaked around the doorway, knitting inwards and obstructing the exit. One vine lashed out at Tasha, sending her backwards clutching her face. She moaned as her fingertips came away bloody. A thin gash ran from her right eye to her chin.

The rats surrounded them.

Ashley threw herself against Greg, who lost his footing and stumbled into Ben's chair, knocking it over. Ben spilled onto the ground, knocking over an LED lantern that rolled away on its side, casting spinning shadows across the ceilings and walls. "Ah, shit!"

AJ stood frozen in shock.

An arm burst through the vines and grabbed for him. It was Samantha, trapped alone in the other room. AJ grabbed her hand and tried to pull her through the vines, but the plant matter was too thick. He could barely see her through all the leaves and thorns.

"AJ, I can't get through. What's happening?" She squeezed his hand desperately. Her wide eyes peered through the narrow gaps still remaining but closing fast.

"Sam! Sam, I'm going to get to you."

"Shit, someone help me," Ben called out. He was panicking, yelling in pain. A dozen rats swarmed over him, nipping at his face and hands as he tried to beat them away. Already he was covered in his own blood. "H-Help me!"

AJ grabbed one of the rats and yanked it off his friend. It was fat and hairy, the size of a man's fist, and it hissed at him as he stared into its evil little eyes. AJ tossed the rodent into the air. "Get the hell out of here!"

Greg stamped on another rat that Ben knocked to the

ground. The sound of its spine snapping was harrowing – the sound of something dying.

Tasha, Ashley, Greg, and AJ all worked together, stamping, kicking, and pulling at the vicious creatures trying to eat their friend, filling the air with blood and the sound of breaking spines. It was sickening in every sense, but Ben was relying on them to save him. He was defenceless against so many sharp teeth.

Greg grabbed Ben's chair and righted it while AJ grabbed Ben under the arms and lifted him back in. Once upright, he was able to roll back out of danger.

A lone rat rushed towards Ashley. She shrieked and cowered. against her chest. Accidentally, the flash on her camera went off. It dazzled the rodent, and gave AJ time to boot the creature into the air.

The remaining rats scurried away.

Ben looked at the bleeding gashes all over his gloved hands and arms as though he couldn't believe it. "AJ, what's happening?"

AJ hurried to the doorway. He could still make out Samantha on the other side, but only just. She stared back at him in terror, and she was forced to pull her arm out of the tightening vines.

A shadow moved behind her, a darkness that seemed to grow and grow. The more it grew, the tighter the vines got, until there was nothing left to see but leaves and thorns.

"Sam! Sam, there's something in there with you."

"What? AJ, what's happening?"

"You're not alone in there!"

Samantha screamed in terror.

AJ clawed at the vines, trying to force his way through. The thorns whipped him, slicing at the flesh of his cheeks, possibly aiming for his eyes – as if plants could attack with intent. He had no choice but to back off. "Sam! Damn it, Sam!"

She screamed again, but this time it was his name. "AJ!"

Greg bumped up against AJ, shaking his head in utter fear and confusion. The expression looked wrong on someone so strong and powerful. "What's going on? What's got Sam?"

AJ stared at the vines, wishing he had laser eyes that could burn them all away. "The druid."

"What?"

"The druid statue. Did you mess with it, Greg?"

Greg frowned and shook his head. "No, I never touched it. What are you saying?"

Samantha's screams faded into nothingness, despite their being nowhere for her to go. AJ shook his head, tears in his eyes. "It's alive."

Greg stared at him. "What is?"

"The ride."

CHAPTER FIFTEEN

BEN WAS IN PAIN, so Tasha was fussing over him. His wounds looked worse than they were, though, and AJ could tell just from looking that the bites were more painful than they were deep. Most of the blood came from the meat of Ben's palms, and he had spread it all over himself as he had tried to fight off the rats, but luckily his gloves had prevented the wounds from going too deep. The green nylon was stained red.

Rats. Did we really just get attacked by rats?

AJ stood staring at the vines covering their way out. They were so thick now that it was as though no doorway had ever existed. Each vine was sinewy and thick, more like a limb than part of a plant. Since Samantha's screams had faded, there had been only a tense, bewildered silence. Everyone wanted to talk about what had just happened, but no one had any words to start the conversation. No one could make sense of it. The only thought crystallising clearly in AJ's mind was that this was all his fault.

Everyone is here because of me. I knew coming here would be dangerous.

But I never expected this.
Still my fault. All my fault.

AJ moved away from the vines, no longer able to face looking at them. He went over to Ashley, who was nearest, and put a hand on her arm. She flinched, then smiled, although it barely qualified as such. "Oh, you made me jump."

"You okay, Ash?"

"I don't understand what's going on. This... this isn't happening, right? It's a joke. Are you setting us up or something?"

AJ wished he could tell her something comforting, but all he could say was, "It's happening."

"Okay, then my next question is: what *exactly* is happening?"

"I don't know."

"This place is haunted," said Tasha, peering over her shoulder as she fussed with her brother's injuries. "That's what's happening. I warned you all. I knew I shouldn't have ignored my instincts."

"Calm down, sis." Ben leant forward and took her hand in his, smearing his blood onto her skin. "We'll figure this out."

Tasha shook her head with an expression that suggested she appreciated his words but didn't believe them for one moment. "You were just attacked by rats, Ben. Rats! You might be dead of tetanus by the end of the week. Unless we die tonight."

"No one is dying," said AJ, and realised he meant it with every fibre of his being. "I don't know what the hell is going on, but we're going to get Sam, and we're getting out of here."

"You said the ride was alive," said Greg. It was part

mocking and part questioning. He clearly hoped AJ had answers that would make sense. He didn't.

It was time for him to mention what he'd seen. He looked at Greg, but he had to will the words to come out of his mouth. "When Ashley interrupted you and me talking in the other room, I noticed the druid statue was gone. If no one here messed with it, then it moved on its own."

Everyone stood silently, digesting what he had just said. None admitted to moving the statue, but Ashley glared at Greg. "More of your stupid pranks?"

Greg looked at her with all seriousness. "I swear on my mother's grave, I didn't touch that statue. I never moved it."

Ashley shook her head as if she didn't believe him, but then she cupped her face in one of her hands and moaned. "I told you that thing was lifelike."

Ben cleared his throat. "You think it might've been an actual person? Some psycho that lives here?"

"No, of course not," said Ashley. "Of course not..." But then she seemed to give it some thought. "Maybe. It felt real."

Tasha had popped one of her dreads into her mouth, but she pulled it out now. "Maybe it's the guy who murdered everyone. I told you his spirit could be stalking this place."

"Or he never died in the first place," said Ashley.

"It's not Donal McCann," said AJ. "He burned here along with everyone else. He's dead. They identified his body. Even his work ID and walkie-talkie."

Ben pulled off his half-eaten, blood-soaked gloves and tossed them on the ground. "Maybe he's not so dead after all. If he worked here, he might have been planning to fake his own death or something."

"Look," said AJ, "when people burn to death in a fire, they don't just turn to ash. They leave bones. The police would've known how many bodies there were. Also, Saxon Hills, and this ride in particular, once repaired, continued to operate for months after the accident. Donal McCann is dead, trust me."

"But he died *here*," said Tasha, "which means his spirit could still be *here*."

Ashley hugged herself. "Don't! Don't freak me out, T."

"Yeah," said Greg, putting his arm around her. "No more ghost talk. Whatever is going on here, it isn't *that*."

Ashley shrugged off Greg's arm and went and stood beside AJ. "What happened to Sam?" she demanded. "It sounded like something grabbed her. You think it was the old man in the other room?"

AJ shrugged. He couldn't prove it, but his mind kept whispering to him that the druid statue had come to life and taken Samantha. Either that, or the statue had never been a statue at all. Could someone really have been living there?

Living here with a swarm of bloodthirsty rats?

Everyone was looking at AJ because he hadn't answered Ashley's question. She asked it again. "What happened to Sam?"

"I don't know. But I'm going to find out."

Thinking fast, he moved over to Greg's portable campfire. The small metal bowl was filled with coals and connected to a mini propane canister. AJ placed his hand beneath the bowl – then hissed at his own stupidity when it burned him. Rethinking, he grabbed the propane canister and dragged the bowl along by the connected pipe. He went slowly, making sure not to tip the bowl and spill the coals.

"What are you doing?" Greg asked irritably.

"Making us an exit." He was about to move the burning coals against the vines when the room flooded with light. A howling wind escaped from the tunnel ahead of the trains and whipped at their clothes and hair. It was like being breathed on by God.

The flame above the coals flickered out.

"Damn it!" AJ fiddled with the ignition, trying to bring back the flames so he could set fire to the vines.

But the wind kept blowing. Kept howling.

Greg grabbed AJ by the shoulder. Once again his pain returned, reminding him that he was hurt. "AJ, forget it. Something's happening."

AJ stood up, grunting with frustration. He was forced to blink at the sudden onslaught of light, and when he looked up at the ceiling, he saw several glowing crystal formations – theming designed to disguise the lightbulbs inside and make the cave seem more 'otherworldly'.

"The power's back on," said Ben, turning his chair slightly and looking around. "You think maybe Sam turned on the—"

AJ cut him off. "Sam didn't do this."

Everyone stood in silence while the world lit up around them. The fishing boats rocked on their tracks as hidden gears engaged. A halo of light shone down on them and the sound of nature erupted. Birds chirped. Distant wolves howled. A malicious voice whispered, over and over again: *Freeennnnzzzy.*

CHAPTER SIXTEEN

"Someone lives here," said Ashley, "and they're not happy that we broke in."

"It's haunted," said Tasha. "I keep telling you."

"No, it's not," snapped Greg.

Ben ran his hands over his head. "Someone is screwing with us."

Although he didn't voice it to the others, AJ noticed that the rats had returned. They milled around the fishing boats, leaping on and off the tracks. They were silent, but every now and then one of them would stop to glare at them.

"It doesn't matter what's happening," AJ said. "We can think about it afterwards. Right now, we need to find Samantha and…" He hesitated for a moment, suddenly unbalanced. Greg reached out to steady him but AJ eased him away. "It's okay, I just got a little light-headed. I was saying we need to find Samantha and get out of here. We can try and make sense of things after."

"Where did Sam even go?" asked Ben. "There's nowhere that room leads to but the queuing area outside. You think whoever took her went into the park?"

"If they did," said Greg, "they could already be half a mile away."

"Then we best hurry," said AJ. "We need to get through these vines. Greg, help me relight the campfire. We can burn our way out, I know it."

Tasha was standing behind him, so she spoke directly to his back. "Are you sure that's a good idea? This place burned down once before and it didn't turn out well. We're trapped in here."

"Exactly," said AJ. "We're trapped, and the only way not to be trapped is to find a way out."

Greg knelt beside the campfire, using his broad back to shield the coals from the wind. AJ hit the ignition switch again, and this time a flame rose to life. He angled the bowl slightly, trying to get the flame to catch on the vines.

A vine lashed out and snuffed out the flame.

Then another slashed at AJ's face.

He stumbled backwards and cursed. "Goddamn it!"

"How is it doing that?" asked Ben, leaning over his armrest. "It's like it's alive."

"It's a plant," said Tasha. "It is alive."

Greg sighed. "Then it's acting a lot more alive than it should be. It just bitch-slapped AJ."

Tasha fingered the slash across her own face. "Yeah, I know how it feels."

Greg tried to light the burner again while AJ recovered, but the vines whipped out again. This time, they entangled the campfire and dragged it inwards. Within seconds, the coals were tied up in the leaves and thorns.

"Okay," said Ben. "That ain't normal. Nothing in my garden ever reached out and snatched shit. We need to take some weedkiller to this thing."

"Or a flamethrower," said Greg.

The vines rustled as if offended.

A chorus of squeaking alerted them all and they turned towards the fishing boats. It should have shocked them to see the rats grouping together again, but they were operating in a daze, devoid of any emotion beyond numb surprise.

Ben spoke in a monotone voice, summing up how they were all feeling. "They're gearing up for round two."

"No," said Ashley. She raised her camera a took a picture without the flash. "They're just standing there. What are they waiting for?"

"For us to climb onboard," said Tasha. "They're leaving a space for us."

The rats had huddled into two separate masses, one to the front of the fishing boat and one to the rear. It left a space in the middle, leading right to the small metal door at the side of the boat.

"They want us to get on the ride?" Ashley let her camera hang from its strap and grabbed a bunch of her red hair. She started wringing it as though it were wet. "They're rats."

Ben wheeled forward a few centimetres. "Apparently, these ones have side-gigs as ride operators."

Ashley let go of her hair and readjusted the strap on her camera so that it hung off her hip. "So, should we ride? We don't, right? That would be crazy."

AJ searched around. There was no chance they were getting through the vines, and there seemed to be no other ways out. Their options were limited.

"I say fuck it!" Greg smacked his fist into his palm. "Someone wants to play games, then let's play."

AJ shook his head, but he wasn't arguing. He just didn't know what to do. "The longer we stand here and do nothing, the longer Sam is in danger. I'm going on the ride alone. There's no reason for us all to take the risk."

"No way," said Greg. "I'm going."

"You need to stay here and look after everyone."

Greg took a step towards the fishing boat. "You stay I'm finding whoever is responsible for this and beating their bloody kidneys in."

Ashley reached out and grabbed AJ, which he thought was surprising seeing as her boyfriend was right next to her. "You can't leave us here. Stay."

"So it's decided," said Greg, moving towards the train.

AJ stopped him. This was his responsibility. "I'm going, Greg. You want to abandon your girlfriend, then that's on you."

Greg looked at Ashley and seemed defeated, but then he changed his mind and shrugged. "She has Ben and Tasha to stay with her."

Ben nodded. "Anyone tries to mess with us, I'll kick the shit out of them."

"Why don't we all go," said Tasha. "Splitting up sounds like the worst idea. We're safer together, surely."

"I'm going wherever you go, AJ." Once again, it was strange that Ashley was clinging to him instead of Greg. Then he considered that he was one of her oldest friends, while Greg had just admitted possibly not loving her any more. It seemed their issues might have progressed beyond the point of repair.

"Okay," said AJ. "We all go."

He moved slowly towards the trains, checking to see if the rats would attack. They stayed where they were though, staring silently.

"So we're actually going to do this?" said Ben. "We're going on a ride that closed down ten years ago, and which may or may not be haunted, because the rats told us to?"

"I told you we shouldn't have come here," said Tasha. "You wanted to experience Frenzy, AJ. Well, you got it."

AJ couldn't feel any guiltier, so he walked forward and took the plunge, wanting to get it over with. He slid through the train's open passenger door and sat down on the bench. The interior had rusted with time, but the cushions were still intact, as they had been earlier when he'd sat inside with Sam.

I'm not going to let you get hurt, Sam. No way.

The rats stood and waited while the others filed in alongside AJ. Ashley yelped suddenly, but none of the rodents had actually done anything to cause her alarm. The boats each had two rows of seats, meant only for two apiece, so it was a tight squeeze for the five of them. Ashley had to sit half on Greg's lap on the rear bench, while Ben pulled himself in beside AJ at the front. Tasha took up the remaining space next to Greg but was forced to leave her brother's chair on the platform. That seemed to bother her more than anything else. "He's helpless without it," she explained.

Ben turned back and frowned at her. "Thanks, sis. Love you too."

"You know what I mean."

"Yeah, I do. Greg will have to carry me on his back if it comes to the worst." Greg grunted, as close to amusement as any of them could get. "I ain't kidding," said Ben.

There was a hiss of brakes releasing, followed by a minor jolt, then the lap bar lowered above their thighs. AJ gripped the metal bar tightly, wondering if it would do anything to actually keep them safe from whatever was to come. "Hold on to your butts," he said. "And keep your arms and legs inside the car at all times."

The boat started forward.

CHAPTER SEVENTEEN

THE FISHING BOAT picked up speed inside the tunnel before slowing suddenly to a crawl a few moments later. The rapid shift in speed threw everyone forward, and Greg cursed disapprovingly. AJ was tempted to squeal with delight though. As much as this whole thing terrified him, he still loved dark rides. And this was the scariest of them all.

The scene on the platform was familiar by now – the starving family. The father was still missing thanks to Greg's shenanigans, and it lay somewhere on its side in the darkness over on the catwalk. Now that the power had come on, a large halogen lamp glared down on them as they passed by the scene, emulating a merciless baking sun. The sound of crickets echoed from hidden speakers, as did the sound of crying children.

Despite being absent, the starving father began to speak as though he were still standing there with his family, his disembodied voice coming from the space where he had been intended to stand.

"*Mighty Woden, save my family, I beg of you. Do not let us perish. Send the rains and fill our fields. To you, I send our finest fishermen. Fill their nets and we shall worship you forever."*

AJ turned to the others. "That's us. We're the fishermen."

"No shit," said Greg.

The halogen lamp pulsated, growing brighter and hotter. It seemed Woden was without mercy, and the starving family moaned. The mother began to move and hug her children, but her animatronic movements were jerky and unnatural. The sound of her weeping was the last thing they heard as the fishing boat lurched forward and picked up speed once again.

"This is stupid," said Greg. "Are we just supposed to ride this thing as though we're having fun? What's the point of all this?"

"Maybe the ride is lonely," Ashley suggested. "Sometimes ghosts and things are sad, right?"

"Yeah," said Tasha, entirely serious. "They envy the living. Maybe this place just wants people to ride it again. That's its purpose."

"And the kidnapping Sam thing is what," said Greg, "just for the lulz?"

AJ shushed them. Bickering wouldn't help them. They were in danger – had been since the moment he'd taken them down that old, abandoned road – and they needed to work together. Maybe the stag back on the road hadn't been intending to hurt them. Perhaps it had been trying to stop them from coming here.

The fishing boat entered the swamp, and this time it was full of water.

Impossible.

Had AJ missed a set of outlet pipes when he'd last been

in here? There had been nothing suggesting the trench could be filled full of water so quickly.

Spray hit them from both sides, a mist rising from the sloped edges of the pretend riverbanks. Dead fish floated on the water, spreading around the boat. A horrid smell came with them.

Ashley held her nose. She then raised her camera and started taking pictures. "Jesus, that stinks. Are those real dead fish?"

"They're props," said AJ, but he wasn't so sure. The dead silvery eyes looked fleshy and real – almost like you could reach out and pop them between your fingers. The smell was *real* too. He reached out, intending to touch one of the slippery corpses, and his index finger was only centimetres away when a shadow glided beneath the water's surface. He recoiled as something reptilian and smooth – pale and sickly – broke the surface of the water before diving back down below. "What the hell is that?"

Ben turned to him, concern in his eyes. "What is it, man? I'm already freaked out enough."

"It's, um, just another prop. Forget it."

The boat rocked as if struck from beneath. Everyone murmured anxiously while Tasha grabbed Ben from behind and held on to him. "When we get out of this, bro, we need to get new friends."

"I hear you."

The river exploded ahead and water cascaded down on the boat. The passengers coughed and spluttered as the icy chill hit them. Then they screamed as a long, slithery mass rose before them.

The beast hissed.

Ben began to pray, which AJ had never seen him do before. Even Greg lost it and started yelling in fear. The boat jolted forward, and the massive snake-like beast crashed back beneath the water, disappearing into the frigid depths.

Tasha was making low moaning sounds like she was in labour. "Oh, oh, God. What the hell was that?"

AJ wracked his brain. He had never read anything online about a section of the ride featuring a giant—

A giant what? What the hell was that thing?

"Was that real?" asked Ben. "Because somebody needs to call the RSPCA if it was. Thing belongs in a zoo."

"Yeah," said Tasha. "Jurassic Park."

No one said anything else. They were all clutching their lap bars and preparing for the next part of the ride. They were scared, but they were unhurt. That was the important thing, right? AJ prayed that every second of terror was one second closer to getting out of there.

The boat picked up speed again, twisting and falling at the same time as it hit the descending helix. They hurtled into the next chamber. It was thrilling. It was terrifying. And AJ realised he was smiling involuntarily. It was all he could do not to put his arms in the air and cheer.

The fishing boat splashed down inside the lower chamber and sent out a tidal wave ahead of them. AJ looked up and saw the thing Samantha had been marvelling at only an hour ago.

Almighty Woden.

The massive stone head glared down at them, his glowing red eyes now pulsating with life. Vines snaked in and out of the ears, nose, and mouth like wriggling worms. Filthy hair hung down almost to the water. The air around the boat tasted stale, like old newspapers left to rot.

Tasha was whimpering quietly to herself, so AJ reached over and took her hand. She held on to him tightly.

Woden began to speak. His rasping baritone rumble sent

ripples across the surface of the water. The bolts and screws holding the fishing boat together rattled.

"WORTHLESS HUMANS! YOU BEG FOR YOUR LIVES BUT THEY MEAN NOTHING. I AM THE MIGHTY WODEN. I CARE NOT FOR YOUR PLIGHT. SACRIFICE, AND SHOW YOURSELVES DESERVING OF MY ATTENTION, AND I SHALL SHOW MERCY. WORSHIP ME OR PERISH."

The massive head snorted, and a foul torrent of steam burst forth from his nostrils. Hot stickiness coated AJ's face, and he had to wipe himself clean.

The boat lurched forward again, heading for the next part of the ride. With his mind in such a mess, AJ couldn't even remember from his research what came next.

Picking up speed, the boat bucked left. Then right. Its passengers screamed as another plummet took them deeper into the earth. It was a fall that seemed to go on forever.

Like falling into Hell.

Maybe that's where we are. Maybe I've led my friends into Hell. Blindly falling forever.

The boat splashed down again and sent up more water. This time they found themselves floating in darkness. Hundreds of stars twinkled overhead against a black background, but there was nothing else. AJ, however, had the unnerving sensation of there being life all around him, like bats swooping past him in the dark and barely missing his face. He had a feeling of *vastness*, like the boat had entered some kind of watery oblivion.

Splashing nearby. Right ahead.

"I can't see a thing," said Ben. "What's happening? AJ, is this part of the ride? I mean from before?"

"I... I can't remember. I know the whole ride is about making a sacrifice to end the famine and save the village.

The middle parts of the ride were about the journey to Woden's grove, where we can make our sacrifice. We... Yes, I remember! We must travel through darkness, fire, ice, and death."

Ben groaned. "Brilliant."

"This would be the darkness part, right?" said Ashley.

Greg tutted. "What d'you think?"

"There's something in here," said Tasha. "I can hear it splashing in the water."

AJ squeezed her hand. "I hear it too. Just stay calm. It's part of the ride. Everything so far has been a show, right? We're all fine."

Ashley spoke in his ear. "Promise me we're going to be okay."

"I promise."

Something broke from the water directly ahead. AJ lost his breath as ice-cold water soaked him. The stars in the false sky expanded, casting more light, and in the ethereal glow a glistening pale column rose in front of them. The same slippery beast as before – a colossal, primal basilisk.

Tasha screamed and clawed at AJ's back.

"It's okay," he shouted back at her. "It's just a prop. It's not real." He had no recollection of this ever being part of the ride.

The hissing serpent glowed in the darkness, capturing the light from the stars above. Its rubbery flesh glistened and its bright yellow eyes bore down on them. Its mouth opened. *Hhhiiiiiiiiiiisssssssssssss!*

Tasha tried to get out of the boat, struggling to remove herself from beneath the lap restraint. AJ had to reach back and try to hold her in place, to prevent her from standing. "Let me out of this goddamn boat," she screamed.

Greg grabbed her by the shoulders and forced her down,

which caused Ashley to yelp as she was thrown from his lap against the side of the boat. "Calm down, T. It's all make-believe."

"Ow, you're hurting me, Greg."

"Just cool it."

"Let go!"

"Get your sodding hands off my sister!"

"Shut up, Ben. She's getting everyone worked up."

"And you're getting *me* worked up. Let go of her now."

AJ caught the glint of Greg's teeth as he snarled in the darkness, but he removed his hand from Tasha's shoulder and Ben relaxed. AJ twisted in his seat and managed to get his hand on Tasha's arm. "It's okay, T. We're all together."

"It's not okay! I want out of this place."

The serpent whipped its head sideways and struck the boat's hull. Everyone screamed, and Tasha started trying to climb out again.

"Oh my God," said Ashley. "We're going to die."

Greg growled. "It's not real, you idiot."

"Fuck you, Greg. Just fuck you!"

"Everyone, stop fighting." AJ couldn't take any more. What was happening to them? They were friends.

Not right now we're not.

The serpent struck the boat again, and this time AJ whacked an elbow against the side wall. Pain flared up his arm and injected itself into his injured shoulder. It was only his fear that kept the pain from sending him into a blubbering mess.

The snake thrashed in the water, sending up more water. Steam filled the air, making it hard to breathe.

"Get us the fuck out of here," said Ben. "Isn't there a GO button on this thing?"

"It's automated," said AJ.

The serpent hissed again, blasting them with its fetid breath. It rose up even taller, looking down on them like a god.

Then it lunged.

The sudden attack startled everyone, and AJ threw his hands up to protect himself. He felt himself scream, but then it got trapped in his throat and he fell to silence. Pain flared through him, a white-hot agony like fish hooks in his veins.

The beast reared back, ready to strike again. Ashley lifted her camera and took a picture. The flash lit up the darkness and, like with the rat earlier, dazzled the serpent. It screeched and turned away. Mercifully, the boat lurched forward, barging the serpent aside. They rocked back and forth, almost capsizing, but they made it through. On to the next part of the ride. The next horror.

AJ was still screaming.

Something was wrong. Very wrong.

Under the dim light of the fake stars, he held up his hands in front of his face. Only one hand entered his vision, however, because the other was missing, a bleeding stump in its place.

AJ threw up over the side of the boat.

CHAPTER EIGHTEEN

THE FISHING BOAT entered a desert scene, cactus hanging over the river from both sides. Vultures squawked hungrily. AJ had resumed his screaming – he had no control over it now. Tasha realised he was hurt, but when she saw the bleeding stump where his right hand used to be, she reacted badly. "Oh! Oh, hell! Shit shit shit! Fuck it!"

AJ stopped screaming and spoke weakly. A shard of bone jutted from his bloody flesh. "H-Help me!"

Tasha turned to the others. "AJ needs help. He really needs help."

Greg leant forward and saw what she was talking about. "Oh! Jesus, is that... is that real?"

"Please, help me. Please!" AJ felt his heart banging against his ribs. His hand was missing. His goddamn hand was just not there any more. A serpent, two storeys high, had bitten it clean off. His vision tilted to and fro and he found himself vomiting over the side of the boat. It felt like he was watching himself rather than experiencing anything first-hand. Was he dying? Was he leaving his body?

"We need to get off this boat," said Greg. "We need to tie off his wrist or he's going to... I don't believe any of this. It's just not... I mean, come on, man!"

"Yeah, okay," said Ben, sounding like he was fighting panic of his own. "How do we stop this goddamn boat?"

The boat was still bobbing up and down and heading along its path, but it did so slowly. The arid scene around them was decorated by baked yellow grass and hot red clay. Flies buzzed around a large rotting carcass somewhere near the back of the room, and a pack of emaciated wolves huddled together at the edge of the river, emitting low growls as vultures perched on a withered tree branch overhead.

"Get off here," said Greg. "There's room."

Tasha protested. "What? We're still moving."

"Only slowly. Come on, everyone out! Quickly!"

Ashley jumped out first as Greg almost threw her. Then Tasha hopped out. Ben and Greg then grabbed AJ around the torso and bundled him over the side of the boat into both girls' arms. AJ did little to help himself, stunned motionless by the loss of his limb. He hit the ground awkwardly and was dragged along on his face as Tasha and Ashley fought to pull him to safety.

Greg jumped out and got AJ in a sitting position. He raised his bleeding stump and told Ashley to hold it there. She did so with a look of horrified revulsion.

"Hey, I need help here!" Ben was leaning over the edge of the boat with both arms outstretched. The boat was starting to pick up speed and it was taking him with it. "Pull me out, Greg."

"Shit!" Greg rushed back to the edge of the river and grabbed Ben under the armpits. With no way of pushing with his legs, Ben was a dead weight. Greg found it hard to heave him over the edge. The lap bar was trapping him.

The boat was about to enter a tunnel at the end of the scene. If he didn't get Ben out now, he would get carried away into the depths by himself.

"Come on, man," Ben pleaded. "Put those muscles to good use for once."

"You're heavier than you look, you fat git."

"More weight for you to shift. So *shift!*"

"Okay, after three. One... two... THREE!"

AJ watched in a daze as Ben flew through the air, yanked upwards by his armpits. In a strange way, he looked like a toddler being swung around by his dad, but then he hit the ground and crumpled into a heap. His chin smashed against the ground, making him swear.

Tasha went to help her brother, but he waved her off and then glared at Greg. "You couldn't put me down a little more gently, man?"

Greg was visibly trembling, which made him somehow seem smaller. "Sorry, you okay?"

Ben rubbed at his chin. It was bleeding from a small penny-sized gash, but with all the rat bites covering him, it was pretty inconsequential. "I might never walk again, you asshole."

Greg managed to smile.

"Help AJ," Ashley urged, redirecting their attention. AJ was ashamed for being a burden, but he couldn't do anything but lie on his side and stare into space. He thought Tasha might have been stroking his back, but he was too numb to know for sure.

Greg hurried over. He examined AJ's bleeding stump while Ashley continued holding it aloft. Blood jetted rhythmically down his wrist. "He's going to bleed out if we don't stem the flow," said Greg. "I'm not wearing a belt. Does anyone have one?"

"I'm wearing one," said Tasha.

"Well, take it off. Quickly!"

Tasha fumbled at her waist and whipped off a funky gem-studded belt. Greg took it from her and frowned. "Not perfect, but it'll have to do."

AJ watched, a spectator of his own fate, as Greg fastened the belt around his bleeding stump and cinched it tight. AJ expected it to hurt, but he only felt a wave of ice run through his arm. He couldn't stop staring at the sharp dagger of bone jutting out from his wrist.

"Hold him still," said Greg. "I need to get this as tight as I can." AJ flinched as a flash of pain finally entered his consciousness, but it was gone so quickly that he wondered if he might have imagined it. "There, okay, think I got it. The bleeding has stopped."

There was a collective sigh, and Ashley looked at Greg. "Is he going to be all right?"

"We need to get him to a hospital."

"That thing was real," said Ben, staring at the river. "That giant snake chewed his hand off for real."

No one said anything.

AJ stared at his stump. Now that it had stopped pissing blood, he could make out the blood vessels and other bits of bone. The appendage no longer seemed like it belonged to him. It was meat.

Meat with a sharp slither of bone sticking out from it. Like a turkey leg.

Ashley stroked AJ's cheek and looked at him. "We're going to get you out of here. Just try to relax."

Greg huffed. "Yeah, just relax."

Tasha hissed. "Shut up. You're not helping."

"Not helping? I just stopped him bleeding to death. Oh, and I dragged your brother's deadweight ass out of the boat."

Ben tutted. "Easy, man."

Ashley shoved Greg in the chest. "Can you please try not to be an utter twat for five minutes? I can't cope with it right now."

Greg opened his mouth to speak, but then he swallowed his words and nodded. "Yeah, okay, I'm sorry. This is all just a bit much, you know? Being an arsehole keeps me from freaking out."

"What should we do?" asked Tasha. "I can't move my brother without his chair, and there's no way out other than the way we came."

"I'm thirsty," AJ muttered.

Greg patted his back. "It's the blood loss. We need to find you some fluids."

"What do we do?" Tasha asked again.

"I don't know! I have no fucking idea. If I start to think for one second about what's actually going on, I end up questioning my own sanity. We're trapped in a sodding theme park ride with a life of its own and my best friend just got chewed up by a goddamn river monster. I have no idea what to do. We are in deep, deep shit."

Tasha lowered her gaze. "Sorry. You're right. This isn't on you, Greg."

"It's on me," said AJ. "I'm sorry. I just... I just wanted to see you all one last time."

Greg grunted. "You're going to America, not the moon. We'll still see each other. Hell, we get out of this, I'll visit you in the States every chance I get. Bit of sun, sand, and Yankee pussy. Count me in."

Ashley slapped him. "You complete and utter shit. To think I wanted to marry you."

Greg held his face in shock. "I... shit, I was just making a joke."

"Some joke," said Tasha, shaking her head in disgust.

"Come on, guys." Ben waved a hand at them all. "Let's not lose it with each other, okay? Your relationship issues are not really the priority right now."

"I'm not going to America," said AJ, making everyone look at him. Now that the words were out of his mouth, he couldn't stop himself from adding to them. "I never got offered any deal to wrestle in the big leagues. An agent came to watch me, that much is true, but I blew my chance. I dropped Dillon and broke his arm. I chopped Tractor until he was bloody in the ring. Then, after the show, Tractor and I came to blows in the locker room. I knocked him right on his fat ass the exact moment the agent walked in to speak with me. He said I was a dangerous amateur, and a disappointment compared to the things he'd heard." AJ huffed and shook his head. "Any other night, I would have brought the house down and got that offer to wrestle in the big leagues. That night... Everything went wrong."

Greg frowned. "You never make mistakes in the ring. What the hell happened? There's something you're not telling us."

"I went blind."

Ben shuffled closer on his butt. "You what?"

AJ felt tears brimming, which felt like yet another betrayal by his eyes. "My vision went, and all of a sudden I was blind. I'm *going* blind."

"Like your mum?" Ashley looked at him, horrified. "You have the same thing?"

"Leber's hereditary optic neuropathy. I went to my doctor the day after the match. I got the result a couple of days ago. I have it."

Ben lowered his head. "I'm sorry, mate. That's shit. Really shit."

AJ sighed. "This weekend might just be the last clear memories I have of you guys. I wanted it to be special."

"That's why this has all been so important to you?" said Greg. "To make a few memories?"

AJ nodded. "When my mum first went blind, she stopped being who she was. She became this useless lump that couldn't do anything for herself. She was a burden I couldn't escape. Now I'm getting what I deserve for being so selfish. I'm going to be a burden too, and you're all going to go on with your lives and forget about me. And I won't blame you at all."

Greg actually seemed to have tears in his eyes, but as much as he appeared to be sad, he was angry too. "Are you really that much of an idiot? We love you, man. If you're going to go through this, then we're all going to be there with you. You should have just told us. I knew you were full of shit about getting an offer to wrestle abroad. Tractor told me what happened with the agent. You'd be lucky to get a wrestling gig in *this* country after knocking out a promoter."

AJ looked at him. "You knew?"

"Of course I knew. I see Tractor and his guys all the time, don't I? You really think I wouldn't have heard about it if you'd got some great offer from an agent?"

"W-Why didn't you say something?"

Greg shrugged. "You're my mate. I'm not about to

embarrass you. I figured you had a reason for lying. Didn't expect this though. I'm sorry, man."

"Me too," said Ashley. "I know how frightened you've always been of your sight going like your mum."

AJ felt a tear strike a path down his cheek. "I always knew there was a chance. It was only denial that allowed me to get up every morning and face the days. It's been like this sword hanging over my head. Now it's finally fallen and the lights are going to go out."

Greg put his hand on AJ's shoulder. "Is there anything they can do for you? I mean, medicine's moved on since your mum lost her sight, right?"

AJ shrugged. "I don't know, maybe. Things haven't progressed to that stage yet. I've only just got the diagnosis." He held up his bloody stump. "I guess I have bigger problems for today."

"I'm going back to the camp we made," said Greg. "I'll grab some food and water, and the first aid kit I brought in my rucksack. Then I'm going to kill whoever is responsible for this."

"You shouldn't go off on your own," said Ashley. "What if you don't come back?"

"I will, I promise." He stood up, then eased Ashley up to stand beside him. "I'm sorry about what you heard," he told her. "I'm a twat, I know."

"You said you didn't love me any more. Is that true?"

"No. I *do* love you. I'm just not sure what that means right now. Once we get out of this place, we can talk properly."

Ashley didn't look happy, but she gave a nod. That was all Greg needed to plunge into the knee-high river and begin wading back the way they had come.

"Be careful, man," Ben shouted after him. "That thing

that attacked AJ is in the next room. I think it's a bad idea you walking off on your own."

Greg slowed a second, as if he had forgotten what would await him and now realised his stupidity, but then he rediscovered his resolve and continued wading towards the tunnel. "If I see it, I'll come back, but the mood I'm in right now, it would be better off hiding from me."

"Maybe you should think about this?" Tasha shouted after him. "There's no good you getting hurt as well."

"If I don't get some supplies, we could lose AJ. I'm not going to risk that."

Nobody said anything else. They watched Greg go.

"It should be me," said AJ. "I should be the one going to get help."

"Yeah, well..." said Ben. "Welcome to the club. Some guys are heroes. Other guys have to sit and watch."

AJ frowned. "What are you talking about?"

He chuckled. "My two best friends are Hulk Hogan and Arnold Schwarzenegger. You have any idea what it's like going down the pub with you and Greg? There's a reason I've been single a long time."

AJ cleared his throat, not knowing how to take his friend's comment. "Sorry, I thought you had game, man. You have women eating out the palm of your hand most nights."

"Yeah, but they never leave with me, do they? I can crack a girl up, but I can't get one to open up."

"That's gross," said Tasha.

"I didn't mean it like that, sis. I mean girls are just uptight around a guy in a wheelchair. They toy with the idea of being that lovely, sweet girl who doesn't see the chair, but then they become a fantasy of themselves rather than anything real. They miss the point that I want a girl that doesn't have to be anything but herself with me. I don't need a goddamn saint."

"Ben…" Tasha moved over to her brother and rubbed his back, but he shrugged her off.

"Sis, I love you more than anyone, but it's like AJ said about his mum – I'm a burden. You shouldn't be sharing a flat with your thirty-year-old brother. You should be backpacking around the world or sleeping around."

"Hey!"

"I just mean you should be having fun. Not stuck watching *Peep Show* reruns while you wait to pick me up from physio. It's not your fault I was born with a damaged spinal cord."

"Why are you saying this?"

Ben looked at her like she was stupid. "Because we're going to die. You said this place was all wrong. I should have listened to you."

"I had a bad feeling, yeah, but deep down I didn't believe anything this bad would happen. I was just freaking out."

"No, sis, you have a gut instinct about these things. You always have. It's your superpower."

She huffed. "What's your power then?

"I can take really hot baths. The world will be a worse place without me."

"Stop talking like that. We're making it out of here."

AJ couldn't listen to them any more. Talking wasn't going to help them. Surprisingly, he found strength and climbed to his feet.

Ashley fussed over him. "Hey, sit back down. You're hurt."

"I am, which is why we need to get out of here. I need a hospital. If my wrestling career wasn't over before, it is now, but I would still like to live."

"Greg's already gone to get help. We should wait for him."

"And we will, but we should be doing something in the meantime. Come on, let's check this place out while I'm still able to stand."

Tasha looked at Ben. "You need anything?"

"Nah, go lend AJ a hand. He needs one."

And so they started searching. No one had any idea what to look for, but a way out was priority number one.

CHAPTER NINETEEN

THE EDGES of the desert scene were lined with beige-painted cement. Sand had been mixed in with the paint to create an image of desert rock, but up close the facade was less convincing. You could see the creases between the different sections of wall.

Ashley was talking to Tasha while they searched. Every now and then she stopped to take a picture. "So, these vibes you get? What are they telling you now?"

Tasha huffed. "That something lives here and we're trespassing on its territory."

"You feel there's a, um, spirit or something?"

"I don't know. I just feel like..." She turned and peered around. "Like we're being watched."

Ashley nodded. "I feel that too."

"Hey, guys!" AJ shouted over to them. "I think I've found something."

Ashley and Tasha hurried over, and he pointed to the narrow gap in the wall he had found.

"What is it?" Ashley looked at him, confused.

"I think it's a fire escape."

Ashley's eyes went wide. "Wow, you found an exit?"

AJ ran his fingers over the gap, feeling it widen towards the bottom. "Maybe. When they rebuilt the ride, they made sure to rectify their mistakes by adding several new fire exits. This must be one of them."

Tasha nodded excitedly. "And it should lead outside?"

"Maybe. I'm going to need your help. It's probably rusted shut by now."

"I'm all yours, Bright Lights."

AJ used his remaining hand to grip the edge of the gap while Tasha and Ashley slid their smaller fingers into the narrower space towards the top. Right away, something began to creak. Behind the cement facade was some kind of steel doorway.

"It's opening," said Ashley. "The gap is widening."

"Pull harder," AJ told them. "We're getting out of here."

"Sis, you need to hurry up."

Tasha looked back, and then she let go of the opening with a gasp. AJ felt the gap narrow as they lost a third of their strength, and he swore as he was forced to let go. He tried to see why Ben was shouting to them.

Holy shit!

The previously inanimate wolf statues had been replaced by something living. Something flesh. The three emaciated beasts, wide and bony at the shoulders, were closing in on Ben, snarling and growling. Ben shuffled towards his sister, but the siblings were cut off from each other by the largest of the wolves. Despite being starved, the animal stood a full four foot high.

Ashley backed up against AJ, and instinctively he went to grab her with both hands. The pain in his bloody stump was dizzying, and a wave of nausea flooded through his guts. He fell onto one knee.

Ben whirled his arms to keep the wolves at bay, but he was wounded prey at their mercy. His sister was anything but defenceless though. Tasha booted one of the wolves in the flank so hard that it yelped and jumped away, leaving an opening that she used to make it to her brother. She positioned herself over him, shielding him from danger, and when a wolf snapped at her ankle, she swore and managed to kick it away.

AJ was forced to shove Ashley aside in order to go help his other friends. The three wolves were circling Ben and Tasha in an ever-shrinking circle. A noose.

He needed to save them before it was too late.

AJ leapt into the air and delivered an A-Kick. As much as it might have been choreographed in the ring, it was a hard, impactful kick, and this time he didn't pull it at the end. The kick sent the smallest of the wolves tumbling all the way into the fake river, where it proceeded to splash around in a panic.

Take that, you damn dirty dog.

The largest wolf pounced at AJ, but he threw himself into a forward roll and avoided it. He straightened up beside Ben and said, "Get your arms around my neck."

Ben wrapped his arms around AJ's shoulders, allowing him to deadlift his friend. Tasha grabbed his legs, and together the three of them scurried over to the fire exit at the back of the pretend desert.

Ashley swung her heavy camera by its strap, warding off one of the wolves stalking her. With her swollen ankle, it was hard for her to balance and fight. "Bugger off!" she shouted. The wolf snapped at her, baring a pair of rotting brown fangs. AJ dropped Ben and turned to help Ashley, shoving her out of the way just as the wolf pounced. Its jaws came down over his stump.

He bellowed in agony.

Tasha gave the wolf a kick in its undercarriage and it backed off before it could tear into any more of AJ's flesh. Blood spilled from his stump, the wound reopened, and he had to suck in the pain to keep his mind focused. "G-Get back to the door," he said. "We need to get it open."

The girls shoved their hands back into the gap while AJ joined them, keeping his eyes on the approaching wolves. The beasts had reformed as a threesome, but they were wary now – unable to get at Ben's easy meat. They would come, but they would come slowly.

AJ got a grip on the edge of the hidden door. With mortal panic running through him, his muscles were bulging with life, and he managed to pull harder than he had before. Both girls joined in and helped him.

Metal screeched, dragging along the cement floor. "It's coming!" said AJ. "Keep going."

"Hurry up, guys," said Ben. "These bitches look hungry."

AJ heaved. A growl at his back caused him to glance around. He threw a swift kick at the wolf and sent it away, but it the distraction caused him to lessen his grip on the door. It closed up again.

"We can't hold it," said Tasha. "It's stuck."

"We have to keep trying." AJ redoubled his efforts and the door began to open again. He realised that, in addition to the sound of the door scraping across the ground, there was the squealing protest of springs. The hinges were designed to close automatically. A typical fire door. The door hinges had rusted almost solid.

"Don't stop!" AJ yelled. "Keep pulling." With only one hand, and having lost a lot of blood, he was struggling to hold on, but he wasn't about to quit.

"I-I can't hold on." Ashley was thrashing her head,

thick veins bulging in her slender neck. Her frizzy red hair was in her face and she couldn't use her hands to move it away. AJ could see her willpower reaching its nadir.

He shook his head at her. "Don't!"

"I can't!"

"Guys!" It was Ben. "You have to get out of here, right now."

AJ chanced a glance at the wolves. They had crept within leaping distance again, and if they coordinated their attack, they would have their jaws around all three of them any second. It was now or never.

"Pull!" AJ locked his jaw.

The gap was now wide enough to pass through, but Ashley was still thrashing her head and gritting her teeth. "I... can't..."

AJ saw her give up. Saw the spark of defeat in her eyes. Her hands came away and the weight in AJ's hands increased. He pulled as hard as he could, but the opening started to close. "No! No!"

Their last chance had just disappeared. If Greg hadn't left, his strength might have saved them. AJ was too weak.

Suddenly the weight in his hands melted away.

The passageway stayed open, barely wide enough to get through. Ashley turned to face the wolves. How was the door still open? Why hadn't it slammed shut?

Tasha screamed.

Ben looked grim. Not in pain, as anyone else would've been, but grim in an emotional way. He knew what he had just done. "G-Get out of here, guys," he told them.

AJ couldn't believe what he was seeing. When the passageway had started to close, Ben had shoved both of his legs into the opening. They were now crushed together inside the gap, jamming the passageway open like a giant doorstop.

AJ swallowed a lump in his throat. "B-Ben, we need to free you."

"Get out of here. Take my sister and get the hell out."

Ashley kicked at a wolf, and cried out as it managed to nip her bad ankle. She swung her camera, cracking it off the animal's skull and knocking it for a loop. Ashley went to deliver a killing blow, but one of the other wolves bounded into her mid-swing and the she lost her grip on the strap. The camera went sailing away into the sand. She staggered back, groaning in misery. She had started to bleed, and the two other wolves, sensing their prey was desperate, bent down and prepared to launch a joint attack.

AJ did what he had to do. He grabbed Ashley and manhandled her, bundling her through the opening before she had a chance to complain. Next, he grabbed Tasha and moved her behind him. "Get through the gap, T."

"We need to help Ben."

AJ kicked the wolf that had nipped Ashley in the snout and managed to daze it, then threw another kick at the largest wolf – but missed. It reared back and snarled. He glanced at Ashley while he had a second. "Go, now!"

Ben repeated the command. "Now, Tasha. Get gone."

AJ had to turn and shove Tasha as it became clear she wasn't going to leave her brother's side. There was no helping Ben, but perhaps AJ was the only one who realised it. His legs were mangled beyond repair, knees crushed together like a pair of cracked eggs. The edge of the opening had cut right into his thigh. Blood was already soaking through his jeans.

Tasha finally passed through the gap to join Ashley on

the other side. AJ heard the two girls crying and comforting one another.

"AJ, get out of here, man," urged Ben. His face had turned pale and sweaty. He might not feel it, but he was losing blood quickly.

"I can't leave you." AJ kicked out at the largest wolf and missed again. The two smaller wolves had backed off, as if they wanted to let their leader handle things.

"I'm screwed, man. You need to get my sister out of here. Then you spend the rest of your life keeping her safe. You owe me that."

AJ backed up towards the exit, wanting to keep the wolves from making it to his defenceless friend. "Why? Why did you stick your legs out?"

Ben shrugged nonchalantly. "It's about time these useless things did something. Look, I can't say I was thinking in the moment. I saw the door closing and—" The widening of his eyes was enough of a warning.

AJ turned just in time to see one of the smaller wolves attacking from the side while he was distracted with the one directly ahead. "Clever bitch!"

The wolf knocked AJ to the ground and mounted him. It bit at his neck, but he managed to keep it at bay with a forearm beneath its chest. In the corner of his eye, he saw the other wolves pacing excitedly.

AJ pulled a leg up and around. Using his flexibility honed by years in the ring, he was able to hook his ankle around the back of the wolf's neck and trap the animal against his chest. He squeezed.

The wolf whimpered and tried to back away, but its fur and ear cartilage bunched up and refused to slide out of the noose AJ had made with his leg and arm. AJ squeezed harder, his entire body crying out in pain. His shoulder felt like it was coming apart.

The other smaller wolf snapped at AJ's face, but he was able to shimmy out of the way on his back. He wouldn't be able to avoid those gnashing teeth forever though.

The trapped wolf went limp beneath his leg. If it had been human, AJ might have suspected it was faking, but he had to risk letting go. Thankfully, as soon as he let go, the wolf flopped lifelessly to the ground, unconscious or perhaps even dead. He'd never choked out a dog before.

AJ tried to get up, but the large wolf pounced immediately and knocked him back to the ground before pinning him. Ben cried out, but that was all he could do. "Hey! Hey, Fido! Get your dirty paws off him."

AJ rolled back and forth, trying to throw the animal off, but it was too heavy – too muscular. Savage.

AJ's shoulder burned. He was losing all feeling. His upper body strength was faltering and his reserves were almost tapped out. The wolf's jaws were getting ever closer to his throat.

"Wow, hey, what the hell is going on here?"

AJ turned his head. "Greg?"

Greg was standing on the catwalk at the beginning of the desert scene. He looked shocked. He had every right to be.

"Greg, help!"

To his credit, Greg came running. The smaller wolf tried to stand in his path, but he tackled it to the ground and punched it in the face. AJ almost chuckled at the absurdity of seeing that, but the large wolf finally got its jaws around his throat and suddenly he could feel nothing but mortal terror. His ability to breathe disappeared.

Air stopped making its way into his lungs.

He couldn't even cry out for help.

Ben called out on his behalf. "Greg, hurry the hell up!"

Greg faltered when he saw Ben's mangled legs sticking into a gap in the wall, but then he saw AJ was in serious trouble. He grabbed the wolf from behind, like a man hugging his dog, but this dog was refusing to drop its prey. "Let go, you mangy sonofabitch."

AJ's vision began to spot with stars and black patches, all twinkling right in front of his nose. Greg beat at the wolf, punching the sides of its head.

"Kick the fucker in the balls," Ben shouted.

Greg looked back over his shoulder, then shrugged, as if to say, *yeah okay, why not?* He hopped back, planted his feet squarely, and then swung a kick right between the wolf's splayed back legs.

The wolf let go of AJ's throat instantly, and released a howl towards the ceiling. AJ shoved the animal away from him and gasped for breath.

The wolf loped away, yowling miserably. The smaller wolf headed after it, nuzzling at its neck. The third wolf was still unconscious on the ground.

Tasha put her head through the gap in the wall. "Come on! Quickly, before they come back."

AJ couldn't get up. His shoulder was molten lead, and his bloody stump was spitting fire. His throat felt like it had been ringed with hot ashes. Greg seemed to realise this because he got AJ's arm around his neck and hoisted him upwards before dragging him over to the gap.

"Come on, mate, I got you." Greg shoved AJ forward into the gap. It was a tight squeeze, and Tasha had to pull him from the other side, but eventually he made it through, collapsing to the ground at Ashley and Tasha's feet. He lay there on his side, panting. His mind flashed with memories of Dillon, and he wished he could revisit that moment. Everything had started going wrong then.

Greg already had one leg through the gap, but he was struggling to fit the rest of his large body. "I-I don't think I can make it."

"Yes, you can," said Ashley, and she hobbled forward and grabbed him by his bulbous arm. Obviously, she couldn't overpower him – not even close – but the added impetus allowed Greg to push himself harder into the gap. He managed to get his hips through, and then he dragged his trailing leg.

All of this he did right over Ben's prone form. He was still lying half in and half out of the gap. "Don't mind me," he said, although it lacked the usual zest his wisecracks typically contained.

"Sorry," said Greg, and then he started angling his wide back and shoulders. It was the hardest part of the manoeuvre, and it took both Tasha and Ashley to help him defeat the laws of geometry.

Finally, Greg's massive frame slid through the opening. He crumpled to the floor in relief beside AJ and started to say something. "You lot want to tell me what the hell is hap—"

Ben yelled.

It jolted AJ enough for him to make it back up to his knees. He crawled over to the opening with Tasha right beside him and the two of them stared back out into the desert scene.

The wolf that AJ had choked unconscious was starting to recover. It rose gingerly to its feet, malicious eyes fixated on Ben – trapped prey. Ben flailed his arms and tried to scare it away. It didn't work.

The wolf pounced.

Tasha screamed. So did Ben.

The wolf cut off Ben's voice as it tore into his throat and thrashed its head back and forth. Tasha started to climb back through the opening, but Greg pulled her back. "Let me! Ben, hold on."

Ben let out a gurgle, and AJ saw blood soaking the wolf's muzzle. He rubbed his own aching throat and realised just how lucky he'd been not to have had his jugular opened. The larger wolf had been toying with him – savouring the kill.

Greg couldn't get back through the gap, and Tasha yowled a high-pitched plea as the other wolves returned to join the kill. Ben's feet began to shuffle on their side of the door, but it was no miracle. The wolves were merely tugging at his body, fangs buried in his arms and neck. His legs began to slide through the gap, flesh slicing away along the edges. Tasha grabbed one of his feet, but his trainer slipped off and she fell backwards.

AJ threw himself into Greg, knocking him away from the opening just in time to keep it from slamming shut on him as Ben's legs removed themselves. He hit the ground and gasped. "That was close!"

Before AJ could say anything in reply, Tasha started beating him, screaming in his face that she wished he was dead. "You should be the one out there. You should be the dead one."

AJ couldn't say anything, because in his head he was agreeing. *It should be me.*

CHAPTER TWENTY

Greg and Ashley pulled Tasha away, but she kicked and clawed, trying to get another shot in at AJ. "You fucking brought us here. Ben is dead because of you!"

"Easy," said Greg. "How could he have known?"

"I told him! I told you all. We should've turned back as soon as that deer blocked our way."

AJ lay on his back, bleeding. "You're right. If I had..." He sighed. "You're right."

She turned away in disgust, sobbing into Ashley's chest. AJ stared at the narrow gap in the wall. The sound of their friend – Tasha's brother – being eaten alive on the other side by wolves was soul-destroying. Crunching bones and wet splatter.

Greg knelt and examined AJ's stump. He seemed concerned but didn't express it. He just recinched the belt and said, "We need to get some fluids in you or you're going to keel over from dehydration. How do you feel?"

AJ huffed. "Are you really asking me that? I'm not sure how I'm still breathing to be honest. Adrenaline, I suppose. We need to find Sam."

Greg looked down at his hands as if something AJ said had upset him.

"What is it?" AJ asked.

"I don't think we're ever getting out of here. This place, it's all wrong, man."

"I think we all understand that, but there has to be a way out. We just have to find it."

Greg shook his head. "I don't think it's going to be that easy."

Ashley glared at them from over Tasha's trembling shoulder. "What are you getting at, Greg? Did something happen when you went back? Where are the supplies you were meant to fetch?"

"I couldn't get them."

"Why?"

"Because as soon as I tried to make it past the room with the starving family, I ended up back here. I made it through the area where AJ was attacked by that... *thing*... but when I walked through the rest of the ride in the direction of the room we left everything in, I ended up back where I started – except you were all being attacked by wolves this time."

Tasha sobbed.

"You just got turned around," said Ashley. "It's dark. Frightening."

Greg shook his head. "I wasn't lost. I followed the walkway in one direction the whole time. I was moving through the rooms, one by one, but I found myself back in the desert with you lot being attacked by wolves. What the hell was that about, anyway? They were just statues when I left."

"They came alive," said Ashley. "AJ found a way out and they attacked us."

"They came alive?" Greg didn't sound as if he was questioning her, more that he was questioning reality itself. AJ understood how he felt.

"None of this should be possible," said AJ. "Ben can't actually be..."

Tasha wheeled on him again. "Well, he is! He's fucking dead. My brother is..." She broke down in tears. "He's gone!"

"I'm so sorry, Tasha. Ben was my best friend. I... I loved him."

Tasha nodded and wiped away snot on the back of her arm. She no longer seemed angry, just *broken*. "He loved you too," she muttered. "That's why he sacrificed his own body keeping our escape open."

Greg frowned at AJ, seeking confirmation. "Ben trapped his own legs in the door?"

AJ nodded. "We wouldn't have made it out of there if he hadn't done what he did."

Greg looked like he'd just been slapped. "Jesus, Ben..."

AJ could barely believe it either. He studied the fire escape they had come through and saw that it was a heavy metal frame affixed to the back of a cement facade. As suspected, the whole thing was corroded, and it hung awkwardly on warped hinges.

The room they were now in wasn't much more than a corridor. There was a mildewy sheet of paper on the wall housed inside a discoloured plastic frame – some kind of certificate or former staff notice. It was impossible to imagine that this place had ever had staff walking around it, bored and waiting for knocking-off time. That this place had ever been normal.

"Why is this happening to us?" Ashley hobbled away from Tasha and sat down on the floor. Her bare ankle was now both swollen *and* bleeding. "Why does this place want us dead?"

"Evil doesn't need a reason," said Tasha. "The way those people burned to death here would have left their spirits angry. Angry that they had their lives cut short. Angry that they never got to say goodbye to their loved ones. All that anger... it turns into something real. Like a force of nature. This place has been infected with the rage and anger of nine innocent victims."

"Eight innocent and one madman," AJ corrected.

Greg studied her. "You really think that's what's going on here?"

"What else could make statues come to life? Or summon giant snakes out of fake rivers? How d'you explain ending up back with us instead of at the entrance where you should've been?"

Greg shrugged. "Maybe we're dead. I always assumed I'd end up in Hell."

AJ frowned. "What? Why? What have you ever done that's so bad?"

"Nothing, but you know what they say about..." He shook his head. "Nothing."

"No," said Ashley, rubbing at her ankle, but looking at him intently. "What were you going to say?"

Greg shrugged again. "Just that I'm a bad guy. Look at how I've treated you."

"You've treated me just fine. That's why I wanted to get married, dumbass."

"Really? You want to marry me? Even though we barely see each other?"

Ashley clutched her hair and started bunching it together. She seemed suddenly evasive. "Well, you're always at the gym, aren't you? It's your career. And I have my photogra—"

"It's not my job to be there twelve hours a day. I go there

so that by the time I get home, I can tell you I'm too tired to do anything or, you know..."

Ashley rolled her eyes and huffed. "Have sex with me. Am I really so repulsive?"

"What? No! You're stunning. I can't believe how beautiful you are."

"So what's the fucking problem? Why haven't you touched me in months?"

"You're just not my type."

Ashley flinched as though he'd slapped her. AJ was a little shocked too. "How can she not be your type? You've been together for years. In fact, when you met, all you did was show the guys down the gym pictures of her on your phone. You thought she was a knockout."

"I was covering."

"Covering *what?*" Ashley was demanding now, getting angry. These issues had begun long before tonight, yet this seemed to be the first time they were truly being aired.

Greg shifted awkwardly, like he was subconsciously hoping he could summon wings and fly away. "That I'm... just that..." He sighed, unable to get out what he was trying to say.

"He's gay, for fuck's sake," said Tasha.

Greg flinched. "W-What?"

Tasha joined them, but didn't sit. She spoke angrily. "You're gay, Greg, what's the big fucking deal? Ben saw you one night getting off with some guy around the back of the library. The physiotherapy clinic is right on the corner. He saw you after one of his evening sessions. It was a shock, he told me, but we both decided it wasn't our business. He was good like that. Never judged a soul. Now he's dead."

Greg was mortified. It looked like his eyes might pop out of his head. Ashley had the exact same expression. "Is it true?" she asked him, gawping like a fish between words. "Are you... are you bisexual?"

Tasha groaned and turned away.

Greg swallowed. Then, all at once, he seemed to deflate. "I don't know. I've always been a bit mixed up about it all. When I got with you, Ash, I really was attracted to you. I thought I'd just been going through a weird phase that was starting to end. A lot of guys get confused in their teens and early twenties, right?" He glanced at AJ, and AJ shrugged as if to say, *sure*.

"So what happened?" Ashley demanded. "How long have you... How long have you been making out with guys round the back of the library?"

"He was just a mate. A nurse at the clinic Ben went to. I should have thought about the risk. Maybe it was the risk of being found out that appealed. I've always been too much of a coward to come clean voluntarily."

"Fine," said Ashley. "How long has it been since you decided you didn't want to be with me then? That you didn't love me?"

Greg shook his head at her vehemently. "Ash, I love you to bits. I love you more than anyone. But I've been having these feelings for a while and they're not going away. The longer we've been together, the more *trapped* I've felt." Ashley rolled her eyes, obviously hurt by the word, but Greg didn't let it interrupt him. "I wanted to be normal. I tried so hard. My dad's voice would always bounce around inside my head. *Faggots go to hell. Queers need a kicking. Fucking bumboys.*"

Tasha was still angry, but she softened for a moment. "Your dad really said those things?"

"His dad was a real piece of work," said Ashley, compassionate all of a sudden, as their shared intimacy came into play. "He used to knock Greg around."

Greg nodded. "He didn't win any father of the year awards, let's put it that way. Maybe if I hadn't spent my entire life being terrified of him, I might've been a little more open about my feelings. Believe me, the last thing I ever wanted to do was hurt you. You don't think I want to settle down and be married with kids? Of course I do – Christ, it would be so simple that way – but I've been realising lately that it's never going to work. I can't force myself to be happy in a situation that doesn't suit me. And it wouldn't be fair to you either. I'm so sorry."

There were tears in Ashley's eyes as she spoke. "I don't know what's worse. That you wasted years of my life I could've spent with someone who actually wanted to be with me, or that you didn't trust me enough to tell me. If you'd spoken about how you were feeling earlier, I would've listened. I would've been there for you."

"Me too," said AJ. "You should've told me, man. Instead, you've been playing the part of an overly butch muscle head. I could happily have done without the act."

"Can anyone say *overcompensating*," said Tasha glumly.

Ashley chuckled. "We don't know the real you, do we, Greg?"

Greg sighed. "Not sure I even know. And now it looks like there's never going to be a chance to find out."

Tasha leant up against the wall and closed her eyes. "Don't say that. I don't want to die in this shit hole. I can't bear the thought of no one ever knowing what happened to Ben. I need to get out of here."

"Let's just take a breather," said Ashley. "I need a moment, you know? This is all just so..."

Greg nodded and so did Tasha. AJ added to the agreement. "Okay, let's take a time-out," he said. "Then we can keep trying to find a way out of here. Sam needs us to keep trying."

"God, *Samantha*," said Ashley. "What the hell happened to her? We have no idea if she's even—"

AJ cut her off. He wouldn't hear of it. "We're going to find her. If she's still in this place, I'll find her."

Tasha rolled her eyes. "Bit late to be a hero."

"You don't think I tried to save Ben?"

Tasha shook her head and fell silent. She seemed to know she was taking things out on him unfairly. The truth was that there was nothing he could say to make it any better for her; and there was nothing she could say to make him feel any worse.

Ben is dead.

And Sam might be too.

By the end of the night, all of his friends might be dead, and even if they lived, he knew he had lost them forever. Just like he had lost his hand, his life, his career.

And soon, his sight.

He blinked twice, trying to clear away the blurriness.

It only got worse.

CHAPTER TWENTY-ONE

"Okay," said Tasha. "I'm ready to get the fuck out of here."

"Or die trying," said Greg.

AJ's attention had drifted, so the sound of voices startled him. He felt as though he'd been asleep, his memory of the last few minutes fuzzy.

"Does anybody have a plan?" Ashley asked. She had bunched her hair into a loose knot and positioned it over her shoulder. It was nice to see her face in full, even if it was streaked with grime. "Because *I* don't."

"Tasha." AJ wasn't sure why he said her name, but his gut told him she was the one who might be able to give them an idea of what they needed to do to get out of there. "Tasha, if this place is haunted by the people who died, how could we appease their spirits? What would get them to let us go?"

Tasha frowned suspiciously. Perhaps she thought he was mocking her. "Well, um, there's the whole unfinished business thing. Most spirits can't move on if they feel like they have something left to do."

Greg said, "Surely anyone who dies has unfinished business?"

Tasha shrugged. "I'm kinda regurgitating fiction here, so take it for what it's worth, but in theory, if someone dies violently, and their killer goes unpunished, they might want the truth to be uncovered."

"But they found the killer," said Greg. "We know the truth. It was that Donal McCann bloke who worked at the park."

AJ thought about it. "So what unfinished business *would* the people here have?"

Ashley cleared her throat and gave a short laugh. "They never got to finish the ride."

Greg groaned, but Tasha seemed to consider it seriously. "You know what, the spirits here could be in some kind of loop. They might be trying to complete their final task. Maybe finishing the ride would bring them closure enough to move on. It might be why the ride powered up, so that we could finish it for them. Their spirits will be drawn to us. We could act on their behalf."

There was a moment's silence, which AJ then broke. "This morning I would've laughed at you, but now I'm not sure of anything."

"So we need to complete the ride?" said Greg, also sounding like he was willing to accept it. "Now that we're trapped in the fire escape?"

Tasha shook her head in disgust. "All that effort, getting through the gap, Ben dying, we should have just stayed put."

"The wolves would still be out there," said Ashley. "We didn't have a choice."

"The wolves only came when we tried to escape," said Tasha, "because we weren't playing by the rules."

AJ nodded. She was right. "We really are supposed to go through..." he stumbled over his words as dizziness took him for a moment, "th-through the entire ride? It doesn't make any sense. The ride was rebuilt and reopened months after the victims died. Why wasn't it haunted during that period? There were never any reports of strange things happening."

They all looked at Tasha. She shrugged. "Maybe the bad energy took a while to build up – kind of like mould. When people were still coming on the ride, the spirits were probably content. Then it was abandoned."

Greg folded his arms and finally seemed doubtful. "You're saying the spirits are lonely?"

Tasha shrugged. "I don't know any more than you do, except you all keep looking at me like I do. AJ is the one who knows this ride inside out. Ask *him* to make a plan."

Everyone looked at AJ, and he shifted uncomfortably. "Okay," he said, "if we are, um, going to try and finish the ride, we need to pass through the icy flats and then enter Woden's sacrificial chamber."

Ashley groaned. "That sounds pleasant."

"It's not," said AJ, "but it leads to the way out. I think that's where we'll find our answers."

"Why do you think that?" asked Greg.

"Because Woden's sacrificial chamber is where everyone burned to death. Whatever is causing this, it has to be coming from there."

"So how do we get there?" Tasha asked. "How do we get back into the ride?"

AJ turned and looked down the corridor. "Through the next fire escape. After the fire, they added one to every single section of the ride. We came out of this one, but we should be able to get back in through the next. This corridor should run past all of them."

Greg stood up and brushed himself down. "On to the big finale then. It's been great knowing you all."

"We're not dead yet," said AJ, then looked away when he

saw Tasha's eyes burning into him. "I'll go first."

"You sure you shouldn't let me?" Greg asked. "You're already on your last life."

AJ held up his stump, pointing the sharp, exposed bone like he was Captain Hook or something. It smelt foul – clotting blood and open flesh. He could feel it throbbing along to his heartbeat. A heavy exhaustion was falling over him, and even if they got out of this ride, he wasn't sure he could make it much further. Greg would need to go get help, which was why they couldn't risk him getting hurt. "I'll go first, Greg. You make sure nothing happens to Ashley and Tasha."

"Yeah, I can do that. Lead the way, brother."

AJ took a moment to breathe, ensuring he had enough energy to keep going. His first step was unsteady, but those that followed were surer. Nothing about this night made sense, and he had never believed in anything supernatural, but he held on to the hope that their plan would work. They just needed to reach the end of the ride. Then all would be revealed.

The corridor was lit by dusty halogen tubes, but they flickered and blinked out periodically. What was keeping the place powered? Electricity, or bad vibes?

"There's another door up ahead," said AJ as he spotted another metal frame bolted to a layer of cement. Such a thing wouldn't have met today's health and safety standards, but as long as it wasn't welded shut, he was glad to see it.

"And there's another door down there," said Tasha. "Maybe it leads outside."

"Yeah," said Greg. "New plan – we try to find a way outside."

AJ shrugged. "Sure, try it."

Greg hurried over to the door further down, a normal door made from wood with a rusty metal handle. The handle fell off as soon as he grabbed it. "Motherf—"

"Nice going, Greg," said Tasha.

"Hold on, I can get us through this." He reared back, then threw himself at the door. The wood was brittle, and it caved in easily.

A black mass erupted from the wood and drenched Greg. It started moving. Writhing. Greg beat at himself and started to panic. "W-What the hell?"

"Spiders," said Ashley, covering her mouth. "You're covered in spiders."

Greg howled like a child and started dancing frantically. He hit himself so hard he would be left with bruises, and the little black bodies squashed and stained his bare skin. Several crept inside his vest.

AJ wasn't usually afraid of spiders, but in such numbers, he would dare anyone not to be creeped out. Despite his fear, he helped his friend, raking at Greg's arms and knocking the scuttling bodies to the ground. Greg backed away from the door, where thousands more spiders spilt from the cracked wood.

Tasha and Ashley eventually got over their fear and started patting Greg down too. Eventually, they got him clean, but he couldn't help but fidget incessantly afterwards. "I still feel 'em on me, man."

"Th-They're all gone," said AJ wearily. The exertion had drained him. "I promise."

Tasha slapped Greg's arm, and then showed him a black mess in her palm. "Okay, *now* they're all gone."

Ashley made for the door. "Come on then, let's get—"

More spiders erupted from the cracked wood, an endless supply. She leapt back and rejoined the others.

"Okay, okay," said Greg, talking to the ceiling. "We get it, we're not supposed to leave. No more spiders, okay?" He around, as if talking directly with the ride. After a moment, when it was clear the walls wouldn't suddenly speak back to him, he turned to AJ. "Before we go back into the ride, let's just cover our bases. We've been attacked by rats, a giant snake, and a pack of wolves. D'you want to give us an idea of what to expect next?"

"All I know," said AJ slowly, "is that it's a frozen landscape. One of the lifeless plains we fishermen must journey through in order to prove ourselves worthy of Woden's favour."

"So it won't be a spot of ice skating then?" said Tasha.

"Afraid not. Are we ready to do this?"

Everyone nodded, so AJ gripped the handle to the ride's exit and prepared to open it. Greg gripped the edge to help, and together they yanked the exit open. Dust and dirt fell away, and the steel frame dragged along the ground. *Screeeeech!*

"Easier than the last door," said AJ.

"Maybe that's because the ride wants us back in," said Ashley. "Are we sure we want to be doing this? Maybe we should try and find another way out again."

"No more spiders," said Greg.

AJ felt in his gut that trying to escape would be wrong. "What if Sam is still in here?" he said. "We make it to the end of the ride and we can go out through the exit platform. We stay in this corridor and who knows what we'll find."

"Spiders," said Greg.

"Yeah," said AJ, "spiders."

"We agreed to go through with this," said Greg. "Let's just stick to the plan. I'll protect you, Ash, I promise."

Ashley folded her arms, but she nodded. "I trust you."

They opened the door fully, and an icy blast hit them all in the face. Greg, wearing a workout vest, began shivering immediately. "They really worked hard to set the scene, didn't they?"

They entered an icy tundra that could have been sliced from the artic itself. Although Frenzy had been notable for its realism, AJ suspected this was something else. The air chilled in front of their mouths, and the floor was slippery. This wasn't mere ride theming. It was make-believe becoming reality.

A campfire lay ahead, near the river, but it was unlit. A group of people lay around it, frozen solid. AJ noticed, with disgust, that some of the people had been butchered for food. Great slabs of human meat hung on wooden spits above the burnt-out campfire. The smell of it lingered in the icy air.

"Those..." Tasha covered her mouth. "Those look like dead bodies."

"This place is getting more real," said AJ. "Somehow, it's becoming real."

"I feel like we're falling into Hell," Ashley mumbled through a hand across her mouth. Her ankle no longer seemed to trouble her at all. She hobbled along at a speed not far off walking. Fear was a great analgesic.

"So let's start climbing our way out," said AJ. "Look over there."

The fishing boat awaited them. Its side door was open, beckoning them to climb inside.

"I can't even work out what a bad idea is any more," said

Tasha. "Once we get back in that boat, we're going to be helpless."

"We've been helpless this whole time," said Greg.

"I'll go first." AJ trod carefully on the ice, being careful not to slip. He knew once he climbed inside the boat that there would be no turning back. He knew what was coming next. And he was willing to die so that his friends didn't have to.

CHAPTER TWENTY-TWO

The lap bar lowered back into place and AJ realised that the soft padding of the cushions had changed. It was no longer black plastic over plump filling, it was flesh. Soft, warm flesh. The others hadn't seemed to have noticed, and he didn't alert them to it, but all the same, it filled him with dread. The ride had been changing ever since they'd first stepped inside. Ever since the druid statue had come to life.

The air brakes hissed and the fishing boat jolted. Rather than shoot forward, they floated steadily, moving away from the icy tundra and towards a deep black tunnel ahead. Steam erupted from somewhere inside the tunnel entrance, causing droplets of water to dribble from the top of the opening.

"I always dreamed of taking my kids to a theme park," said AJ. "I thought my life would go differently."

"Yeah, well," said Greg. "Life isn't always what we choose."

"Tell me about it," said Ashley.

Tasha tutted at them all. "Seriously, guys. We can re-evaluate our lives later. I'm just focusing on staying alive. Or dying quickly."

The fishing boat entered the darkness of the tunnel.

But it was not all dark.

They passed by a featureless embankment lit only by the soft white glow of the people standing there. AJ quickly counted them and saw eight. Eight people bathed in light steadily floating by. He saw a man in a denim jacket standing on his own. He saw a teenaged couple leaning against one another. They all looked so sad. They all watched without doing or saying anything.

They just watched.

"It's the people who died here," said AJ.

Greg frowned at him.

With a lizard-like hiss, the ghosts scattered. There was a faintly audible residue of sound, like faraway screaming.

"What's happening?" Greg asked frantically.

AJ shook his head. "I don't know."

The water exploded, and by now they all knew what to expect. The serpent broke free of the water and thrashed its head about. It whipped at the fishing boat and everyone ducked.

"Why is this thing trying to kill us?" Ashley cowered in the footwell. "We're riding, aren't we? Isn't that what we're supposed to do? It doesn't make any sense."

"What the hell is it?" Greg asked.

"It's not part of the original ride," said AJ. "It's not part of Frenzy."

"Then what?"

"It's Donal McCann," said Tasha. "If it's not part of the original ride, then it's something else that came to rest here. It's Donal's spirit. His *evil* spirit."

Greg swore. "You're just making shit up."

"No!" said AJ. "I think she's right. We just saw the eight

innocent victims, but Donal was number nine. The spirits scattered as soon as the snake appeared. It's Donal. They're afraid of him."

The snake hissed and threw up more water.

"Please, make it stop," Ashley begged.

Greg rose up and placed himself across her. "It's okay. I got you."

The snake struck again. Everyone ducked, but AJ took a knock on the side of the head that sent him dizzy. If it wasn't for the lap restraint, he might've fallen out of the boat.

Greg swore again. "Why is it attacking?"

"Because Donal McCann was a psychopath," said Tasha. "People don't get better when they're dead. Once a nutcase, always a nutcase."

The snake rose again, fangs piercings the shadows, each one the length of a forearm. AJ knew that one bite could kill any one of them. He couldn't let that happen.

"Donal! Donal, you will not harm these people."

The snake reared back, hissed, but didn't strike. It seemed to study AJ curiously. Was it really Donal?

"Donal McCann, let us go in peace."

Greg grunted. "Really? Your plan is to ask the snake nicely not to eat us?"

But the snake wasn't attacking. It was still studying AJ, seeming to contemplate the situation.

"Donal, we are sorry for disturbing you. We wish only to leave."

"It's working," said Ashley. "It's not attack—"

The serpent struck the boat and almost managed to lift it off the hidden tracks beneath the water. Everyone barely held on, gripping the lap bar for dear life.

"Fuck sake," said Greg. "We need another plan."

"That was all I had," said AJ.

The boat rocked back and forth, still reeling from the hit, but it continued along the river. Somehow, despite the lack of light, AJ felt his eyes blur. His vision was betraying him again.

But right now, he didn't need it.

He forced the lap restraint upwards, pushing with his one hand so hard that either his arm would break or the bar would yield. The bar submitted first. Like a muscle tearing, the bar gave way suddenly, springing upwards and becoming loose.

AJ stood.

Greg tried to grab him. "What the hell are you doing, man?"

"Fighting my retirement match." He leapt from the side of the boat, hoping to make it to whatever platform the ghosts had been standing on. For a moment it felt like he would never find solid ground again. He was just floating through the darkness.

Then he struck something hard. His knees thudded down but at the wrong angle. His body slumped over the edge of some kind of concrete platform with his legs dangling in the river. Although it had been impossible to judge in the dark, he hadn't jumped far enough. Now he was losing his grip, in danger of sinking backwards into the water. He only had one hand with which to hold on, so he dug in with his elbows.

It still wasn't enough.

The serpent could have attacked him, but it had gone silent. The thrashing in the water had stopped.

"AJ," Greg shouted. "AJ, man, I can hardly see you. Are you okay?"

"I... Yeah, I'm... I'm slip—" His words died in his throat as a heart-stopping chill came over him. The darkness lit around him, and all of a sudden he could see clearly. The shadows departed to reveal the image of a young boy. The same young boy who had stood holding hands with his father on the platform only minutes ago.

This is it. This is the moment I die. In a dark ride, abandoned and forgotten. Another grizzly footnote in Frenzy's history.

The boy looked down at AJ. He looked so sad. The kind of sad that made AJ's eyes well up for no discernible reason. The only feeling he could describe was *tragic*.

This boy was tragedy.

It made AJ think of all the beaming kids in the crowd at his wrestling matches. Every night he had put his body on the line for them – for the kids. He risked his health to see young people smiling. Enjoying themselves. Erasing the pain of the childhood he never had himself. This child had never had a childhood either.

The boy offered a tiny hand to AJ. If AJ took it, he would have to lift his good hand from the concrete. He would lose the only thing anchoring him in place.

Greg called out again. So did the others in the boat. "AJ? Are you okay?"

AJ ignored them. He let go of the concrete and threw out his hand. His palm connected with the child's icy flesh and he felt his heart stop in his chest. For a brief moment he was in agony, like his ribcage was about to burst open, but then he was flying through the air, yanked upwards by a monumental force.

He returned to earth softly, as if he were a feather on the wind. He turned to the boy and smiled. "You're Billy Scott?"

The boy nodded. A grin crept across his face.

Then he changed.

The child tiny body erupted, the frail body giving way to a growing serpent. With a hiss, it struck at AJ, but he managed to throw himself forward into a roll as if ducking a lariat in the ring. He instantly twisted back to face the other way.

Seeing the small boy's form possessed and perverted in this way filled AJ with anger. Even now, in the afterlife, Billy Scott was being tortured. "Leave him alone, you bastard. He's nine years old. Nine years old, and you took his life away from him. Adults are supposed to look after children, not hurt them. Children are supposed to play and learn and never worry about anything." AJ was filled with a rage he had never felt before, not even in the ring when pricks like Tractor got on his last nerve. He leapt up and dropkicked the serpent, planting both feet firmly into its flank. The serpent roared, not out of pain, for it was thick and monstrous, but in anger. Anger at having been assaulted by something so tiny and inconsequential. But 'Bright Lights' AJ Star had made a career out of being the underdog. He'd beaten monsters before, and he would do it again. He was Hulk Hogan body slamming Andre the Giant. He was Rey Mysterio Jr taking on Kevin Nash.

No, I'm just a guy trying to keep his friends alive.
That's enough.

The fishing boat was still bobbing along the river, barely visible in the shadows. AJ wasn't sure how much longer it had to go until it made it out of the darkness, but he thought he could see a pair of flaming torches in the distance maybe thirty metres away. He wished it was thirty centimetres.

AJ returned his focus to the serpent, wheeling around and sidestepping. The snake was large and cumbersome. While it fought to keep AJ in its sights, it had to constantly whip itself around. While it was tracking him, it couldn't strike. All the while, AJ's friends continued bobbing towards those distant torches – towards safety.

"That's it, Damien," he said, recalling the name of Jake the Snake's pet. "Keep your beady eyes on me."

The giant snake struck, but it was nowhere near the mark as AJ skipped aside easily. His vision was failing, and the serpent appeared to him only as a blur, but that somehow helped. With no ability to focus on detail, AJ could make out the only thing he needed to focus on, which was getting away from the milky-skinned abomination trying to devour him.

The fishing boat was halfway to safety.

Just a little longer.

AJ dodged again. The serpent whipped itself horizontally and almost took his head off, but he lay flat, as though he had just Irish-whipped an opponent against the ropes. He quickly hopped up and did a cartwheel, bringing himself right up alongside the beast's thick trunk. Out of instinct, he threw a punch, but his fist thudded harmlessly against the rubbery flesh. It succeeded in angering his enemy though, and the serpent lashed out unexpectedly, twisting around like a coiled rope.

AJ tried to spring aside but found himself surrounded by slithery flesh. The serpent's body tightened around him like a noose. AJ bellowed as his body closed in on itself, crushed by the giant constricting serpent. He felt his injured shoulder finally disintegrate into bone fragments and torn muscle. The pain reached a point where it was almost spiritual, like his soul itself was screaming.

The serpent lowered its head to within biting distance of AJ's face. Its burning eyes were full of malevolence, the kind of hatred that came from years of being twisted and tormented. At that moment, AJ knew he was looking into the eyes of Donal McCann. Somehow, his twisted soul had remained inside this ride.

"Why did you kill all those people? Children, teenagers? You couldn't have truly thought you were doing God's work."

There was a flicker of recognition in the serpent's eyes. The words had gone in, caused a reaction. AJ realised he had been fighting this thing as a 'face', dodging and diving to avoid its crushing blows, but that had been the wrong strategy. He wanted to get away from this thing, not fight it, but heroes never ran. Villains retreated.

AJ summoned the 'heel' persona he had honed during his years in the ring. His expression fell into a cocky smirk. All self-doubt drifted away. He shoved his thumb into the serpent's eye, trying to pop it like a pus-filled blister.

The serpent recoiled, unwittingly lengthening its body and allowing AJ to slip out of its grasp. He crumpled to the ground, his entire body broken, bones no longer working in synergy, organs no longer functioning – but he was able to run. And that was all he needed.

In the darkness, AJ spotted a grey blur of shadow – his friends on the fishing boat. They were right at the end of the tunnel, yelling out for him but unable to see him. The light of the flaming torches illuminated their terrified faces. Even Greg looked defeated – not just a blubbering mess, but a ruined man. A man without hope.

AJ pumped his legs, putting every last ounce of remaining energy into his thighs. He heard the snake screeching behind him – felt the ground shake.

It was coming for him.

The serpent was ready to devour him.

AJ made it to the end of the platform and leapt. The

rush of hot air at his back could only have been from the serpent's snapping jaws. Once again, he was weightless, floating through the darkness towards a small cone of light around his friends.

They were the light in his darkness.

His friends.

CHAPTER TWENTY-THREE

AJ HIT THE BOAT AWKWARDLY, knocking heads with Greg. It was such a minor pain compared to the pain in the rest of his body that it barely even registered, and Greg wasn't upset either. He gathered AJ to the safety of the bench beside him, and started grabbing at him desperately. "AJ! Shit, you're okay. I thought that thing—"

"Get down," Tasha shouted.

The serpent sliced its fangs right across the top of the boat. Everyone threw themselves down.

Then they were away. Into the darkness of the tunnel. Away from the serpent and its pitch-black lair.

"There's light," said Tasha. "Thank God."

AJ remained in darkness though. "I can't see," he said. "My eyes."

Nobody said anything. It was a statement that had no obvious reply. Greg changed the subject. "Are we heading to the last room now?"

AJ nodded. "Woden's sacrificial chamber. It's where Donal McCann set the fire. It's where Woden will demand a sacrifice to save the lands from famine."

"What sacrifice?" asked Ashley.

"The lives of the fishermen brave enough to reach the sacrificial chamber."

"That would be us," said Greg.

Ashley chuckled nervously. "But it's just pretend, right? I mean, this whole thing is the story of the ride."

"Yes," said AJ. "There was no actual sacrifice. The fishing boats would just plummet into a large hole, supposedly into Hell."

"I can feel us climbing," said Greg. "I think we're going up a hill."

AJ listened to the gentle *clack-clacking*. "We're on a chain-lift. The sacrificial chamber is at the top."

"It's getting windy," said Tasha.

"I can see something up ahead," said Ashley.

To AJ's relief, his vision started to return. His inherited blindness wasn't something that should just keep coming and going like this, and he wondered if it was actually blood loss or brain damage. Was death closing in on him?

Ahead of the boat, a rectangle of light grew and grew. The final cavern was coming into view.

AJ's mind turned to Sam. Would he find her here?

"YOU HAVE PREVAILED AGAINST THE ELEMENTS, MORTALS. WELCOME TO MY CHAMBER."

Everyone jolted at the sudden booming voice, but it soon became apparent that it was Woden's recorded welcome. It had a slightly stilted delivery that gave away its pre-rehearsed quality.

The boat levelled out at the top of the hill and then entered a chamber larger than all that had come before. AJ knew that it took up the entire upper floor of Frenzy. It was impressive. Even in 2019, it was impressive.

"This was all part of the original ride?" Greg asked. "This must have cost a fortune."

"Like I said" – wearily, AJ looked up at the high engraved ceilings – "it was the... the last roll of the... dice."

Woden's face glared down at them again, as it had done in the lower chamber, but this time it was even more colossal. A giant head from a being tall enough to hold up the sky. It was also more real than the one before. The man-made facade of plaster and cheap stone had somehow transformed into flesh and sinewy vines.

Fire burned all around them, close enough to bathe the fishing boat in an uncomfortable heat, but the majority of the inferno was ahead. A crucible of flame growing from out of the river. A whirlpool of fiery death.

Tasha brushed her dreads back off her forehead and started panting. "So this is where we die, huh?"

"Not dying," said AJ, although he wasn't sure whether to include himself in that. He felt sleepy and cold, despite the fire and excitement. His stump was no longer bleeding, and he could no longer feel his pulse beating through it. Even the exposed bone seemed to have lost colour. It had gone from grey-white to an almost translucent colour.

Blood streaked Ashley face, making her look like a Celtic warrior. Only the fear on her face broke he illusion. "W-What happens now?"

"We save Samantha and get out of here," said Greg. "Look!" He pointed to one side, to a gap in the fire. There, standing on a raised platform, stood the druid from the very first room. The withered old man held Samantha in his arms, unconscious, ready to throw her into the fire.

"THIS IS MY DOMAIN AND NO ONE MAY ESCAPE IT. SACRIFICE YOUR LIVES TO ME WILLINGLY AND

YOUR FAMILIES SHALL SURVIVE. REFUSE, AND ONLY DEATH WILL COME TO YOUR HOMELAND."

AJ couldn't take his eyes off Samantha. She was right there, only metres away. Maybe he could get to her.

Ashley gripped the lap bar. "This is all still part of the ride, right?"

"No" said AJ, he was having to concentrate hard to get his words out. His tongue felt too big in his mouth, like a slab of cold fish. "It's like... like something has taken over the ride, brought it to life. I don't, I don't... I don't think this has anything to do with... Donal McCann. He thought the ride was blasphemous. Wanted to destroy it, not control it. It... It feels like his spirit is trapped here. Not in charge of what's happening."

"He's just hanging around the place dressed as a giant snake then?" said Greg. "There's a perfectly rational explanation for that, I'm sure."

"Not one I can think of," said Tasha.

The boat came to an abrupt stop. The fire flared all around them, increasing the heat in the chamber. Ahead, the crucible of fire spread out, revealing a massive sinkhole in the water. Woden's giant visage began to laugh.

"WELCOME TO AN ETERNITY IN MY GROVE."

The rear of the boat began to rise up, tipping them forward against the lap restraints. The massive whirlpool beckoned them.

"We're going to fall in," cried Ashley.

"No," said AJ. "Not yet."

The hole opened wider. The boat tilted at a forty-five degree angle, perched right against it. They began to creep forward. Falling. But then they stopped.

"ARE THERE ANY AMONG YOU PREPARED TO

SACRIFICE YOURSELVES? OR WILL YOU ALL DIE AS COWARDS?"

"What do we do?" Greg asked.

AJ struggled to hold his head up and it ended up flopping about left and right. "Nothing. At the bottom is the exit room. It's our... way out."

"Unless it's sealed up. You think this place is just going to let us walk out of here?"

"No, I don't. Not unless we figure out what it wants from us."

The boat jolted forward, and it looked like they were about to go down the hole and finish the ride. A whoosh of air hit them in the face, and something clunked. AJ saw a metal pole spring up beside the boat and lock into place. It was the manual brake. Something had engaged it and trapped the boat in place. Keeping them there.

The ride wasn't finished with them yet.

A man appeared in the flames suddenly to their right. He was badly burnt and reached out to them as if begging for their help. "They said I burned them." He spoke with a cracked and ruined voice. "They said I killed them all."

It was hard to see the man's features through the bubbling flesh, but AJ knew who he was looking at. He could almost feel who this man was. "Donal McCann?"

"I never meant to hurt anyone," he said. "This place is evil. I needed to destroy it. I brought the petrol, ready to burn it to the ground. I hid it all in this room. I was going to come back at night. I never meant for them to burn. It wasn't me. It wasn't me! They don't know the truth."

The flames rose all around, licking at the cavernous ceiling. Figures appeared on either side of the boat, shimmering spirits howling in silent agony. The other people who died there.

"It was the boy," said Donal's spirit. "The boy killed us all."

The spirits howled even louder. Then they scattered to the edges of the room as a new spirit entered the flames. It was the young boy who had helped AJ earlier. This time, he didn't seem like an innocent victim. He was a twisted spiral of hate and malice. Evil. A vile odour filled the cavern, and when he blinked, he blinked with the vertical eyelids of a snake.

"It was Billy Scott," said AJ in shock, some of his sleepiness scattering. "H-He was the one who set the fire. D-Donal McCann was innocent."

Greg frowned at AJ. "What are you talking about?"

"Can't you see? Don't you see him?"

"See who? All I see is a shitload of a fire, a massive stone head, and a big bloody hole..."

"The boy," said AJ. He stared at Billy Scott in the flames. The boy hissed, a forked tongue slithering between his lips. "You don't see him?"

"I don't see anyone," said Greg.

"Me neither," said both girls.

AJ blinked, rubbed at his eyes, then looked back into the flames. Billy Scott was still there, glaring like an embodiment of hatred. All of the other spirits were still present, but they cowered at the edges of the room. The druid figure moved towards the hole with Samantha.

AJ threw out an arm. "No! Sam!"

"We have to get her," said Greg. "He's going to throw her down the hole."

"Why?" asked Ashley. "Why?"

AJ managed to tumble out of the boat and make it onto the platform. The heat chewed at his flesh, and he thought he would have no choice but to retreat, unable to bear the agony, but then his body adjusted and the pain became less extreme. Sweat burst from his pores. "S-Sam!"

Greg leapt out of the boat behind AJ, shielding his face with his arm. "Jesus. I'm boiling alive."

"Greg! Get back in the boat."

"No way. You're too weak. I need to help Sam."

AJ felt the weakness in his own legs and couldn't argue. Samantha needed rescuing, and AJ couldn't do it alone. "Come on. Quick!"

They raced along the edge of the platform, heading towards the mechanically moving druid. It was clear that the figure wasn't actually alive. It was an animatronic being wielded by a supernatural force. A tool of evil.

Donal McCann appeared in their path and blocked them. "No! You can't die here. The old one, he needs more souls. You must not die in this chamber."

AJ paused and asked, "Why?" Greg looked back at him confused. He still couldn't see the spirits.

Donal's spirit flickered like a grainy VHS. "You can't die in Woden's chamber. He can have no more offerings. If Billy offers more innocent lives to the old one, he will break free of this place and spread his evil across the land like a plague."

Greg looked at AJ. "Why did you stop?"

"Th-The spirits. They're trapped here. Killed as offerings to Woden. Billy Scott wants to sacrifice us too."

"What? I don't understand."

"This place..." said Donal. "It's a temple to the old god, built by fools who didn't know any better. They used his image without knowing its power. The evil called out to all those who entered, hoping to find a soul dark enough to obey its commands."

AJ swallowed a lump in his throat. "Billy Scott."

"It spoke to the boy. Told him to light the match. The boy is Woden's servant. He can't be allowed to offer more lives."

Greg shoved AJ. "Come on! Sam needs us."

AJ wanted to stay and learn more from Donal, but Sam had no time left. She was stirring in the druid's arms, but he was right at the edge of the platform now, about to throw her in. She had no idea she was about to die.

AJ knew he couldn't climb the platform in time. He could barely stand. He put his hand on Greg's back and pushed. "Go! Save her."

Greg patted AJ's arm and then took off like a rocket. It was a miracle he had any strength left, but Greg didn't stop until his muscles were about to burst.

AJ shambled forward, every step a challenge, and he watched Greg hurtle up the incline, rushing towards the druid. It was unclear whether he would make it in time.

"Come on, Greg! Faster."

Greg blew out his cheeks and picked up speed. He made it to the top of the platform right as the druid stopped at the edge. There was only a split second to act, but he was right there. Right there, about to reach out and—

"Feel the burn, you son-of-a-bitch."

The druid spun around and dropped Sam on the ground. Greg was moving too quickly to stop, so he dropped his shoulder and prepared for a collision. He was going to barge the animatronic villain right off the ledge and into the flames.

The druid stepped jerkily, and quickly, to the left — a stiff-jointed matador avoiding a charging bull. Greg rushed right on by, colliding with nothing but air.

What happened next happened in slow motion. AJ felt himself yelling, but he knew there was nothing he could do.

Unable to stop, Greg hurtled off the edge of the platform. He seemed to run across the thin air for a moment, like a cartoon animal, but then he fell. His large, perfectly honed body disappeared into the fiery chasm and, just like that, he was gone.

Ashley stood up in the boat and screamed Greg's name. AJ fell to his knees, struck in the guts by the sight of his friend falling to his death. Another friend dead.

The entire cavern rumbled. The massive Woden head vibrated and pulsed. It seemed to grow more real – a mirage becoming solid.

To the sound of everyone yelling out in anguish, Sam finally woke up. She was lying on her side, but she rose up on one elbow to look down at them.

The druid watched her from behind.

AJ stumbled forward, knowing he could never reach her in time but unwilling not to try. Sam saw him, confusion in her eyes. "AJ? AJ, what's happening."

AJ felt his body shutting off. His vision began to darken. Once again, Sam was unaware of the danger behind her, and he was standing there, powerless to help.

Sam must have sensed the druid behind her because she turned and saw it. "Oh! Oh, God. AJ, help!"

AJ made it to the edge of the platform, looking up at the sheer edge, wishing he could leap ten feet and get to her before the druid caught her and shoved her to her death.

There was only one thing that could save her.

"Y-You have to jump."

"What?"

AJ stumbled, his vision growing worse. He opened up his arms. "Jump, Sam. Jump now. I'll catch you."

The druid reached down and grabbed her ponytail. It started dragging her backwards. She scrabbled to get to her feet, but she was off balance and unable to get up. The druid dragged her to the edge of the platform.

"No!" AJ was too weak to move. Calling out took the last of his breath.

Behind him, Ashley and Tasha screamed. He glanced back and saw the serpent rising up behind them – Billy's twisted visage. He was about to watch the last of his friends die.

Sam yowled as the druid continued to drag her, but then she fell back down on her haunches as something else appeared on the platform.

Donal McCann appeared and grabbed the druid figure. It released Sam as it was unexpectedly yanked backwards, and she managed to scurry away. It was only a minor reprieve, however, as the possessed animatronic speared its entire arm through Donal's ethereal torso. He might have been a ghost, but the poor man wailed in pain. Then dissipated into nothingness.

The druid turned back to Sam.

Sam scrambled to the edge of the platform. She took only one breath before throwing herself off.

AJ's vision swirled. He opened up his body and prayed. Not to Woden, but to the God he had always known. The God who had replaced ancient evils like Woden.

A sudden, massive weight struck AJ. His lungs flattened, and the wind escaped him as he was crushed against the unyielding ground. He lay there for a second, checking if anything hurt. Everything did, but that wasn't his concern. He felt a body in his arms. "Sam? Sam, are you okay?"

"AJ? I want to go home."

He nodded. "Don't worry. You're going home right now."

Somehow, AJ found the strength to get up. He pulled Sam next to him and bundled her towards the boat. The serpent still rose up from the river, but it was yet to attack. Perhaps it had been waiting for Sam's death that had never arrived. It was staring at AJ with utter hatred in its eyes. "Fuck you, Billy."

The snake lashed out, and AJ shoved Sam into the boat. Tasha and Ashley grabbed her and pulled her to safety.

AJ was too weak to move, which was why the serpent was able to clamp its jaws around his shoulder. He felt the stabbing of white-hot fangs, but he didn't care. He only cared about the three people in the boat.

AJ still had his feet on the ground, and he pushed in the direction of the river. His body rattled like a weightless doll as the serpent thrashed, tossing him this way and that. His friends tried to grab him and pull him onboard, but it was useless.

Sam reached out furthest, managing to touch his cheek. "AJ! AJ, please!"

He turned his head and managed to smile. "Go home, Sam."

Using the last ounces of his strength, AJ kicked out a leg and managed to hit the manual brake on the tracks. There was a screeching grind of metal and the boat crept forward. Just an inch at first, but then it gathered speed like a rolling stone, gliding along the tracks towards the gaping hole.

Sam tried to grab hold of AJ, but the serpent was already yanking him away. The screams of his friends faded as they plummeted down the final, long drop, just as the ride makers would have originally wanted. AJ looked up at the serpent, at the beast that was really a wicked, undead child loyal to the ancient god Woden.

I doubt the ride makers intended this.

CHAPTER TWENTY-FOUR

AJ COLLAPSED TO THE FLOOR, the last of his blood draining out of him. It congealed against the stone as the flames curdled it. The spirits of the place watched him fearfully, but they didn't help.

The druid clomped towards him, making no effort to rush. Why would it? AJ was done for. He would be dead any moment with or without their help.

The serpent recoiled and shrank until it was once again a small boy. Somehow, the child was more terrifying than the snake.

AJ tried to get up, but he stumbled and fell. There was a hole in his shoulder and it stopped him from working, like shoving a spike into the spokes of a gear.

"You're god is dead, you idiot. You threw people's lives away for nothing."

Billy said nothing. He just stared with those hate-filled eyes.

"You'll stay trapped here forever. My friends are gone. They escaped you."

Billy stopped approaching. A malicious smirk crept onto

his lips and he hissed. "I only need one. One more offering to break the bonds that bind us."

AJ's heart stopped in his chest. The pain seized him, but terror kept him alert. He tried to put things together, and all he could think of was that Billy needed to kill a certain number of innocent people. When Ben had died, the icy tundra became real. When Greg had died, the cavern shook and Woden's visage came closer to reality. Would one more death be enough to free the evil god forever? Would AJ's death doom the world?

The cavern rumbled again, and the stone beneath AJ's knees changed. Grass and sinewy weeds began to burst forth and take root. Vines dangled from the ceiling. Bats flittered back and forth.

Billy grinned from ear to ear, his mouth filled with sharp dagger-like teeth. "Behold the return of the god of the forest. Soon he shall go forth and remove mankind's stain upon the grove. Nature shall reclaim this earth."

AJ couldn't be responsible for the end of civilisation. He couldn't allow his murder to be the catalyst for extinction.

Murder. Murder is Billy's offering to his god.

"You can't offer me to Woden," said AJ. "Because I won't let you kill me."

"I already have," Billy hissed. "You bleed out by the second at my hand. Your flesh litters the ground."

AJ wobbled on his knees. He felt his life trickling away with every last drop of blood escaping his body. His heart still wasn't beating in his chest. Despite all this, he smiled and held up his bloody stump, and the sharp bone pointed up at the ceiling. "I told you, I won't let you kill me."

Billy tilted his head and hissed, his forked tongue tasting the air. It was a look that might have been confusion.

"They call this blading, and the kids never see it coming."

AJ jammed the sharp bone of his wrist into his own jugular, going deep and tearing his neck to shreds. The last of his blood arced into the air.

His vision finally deserted him for good. All he could see was black.

And then even that disappeared.

CHAPTER TWENTY-FIVE

SAM PARKED her beat-up Land Rover in the middle of the road and turned off the engine. She hadn't thought about the strange broken-antlered stag in a long time, but once she had started down the neglected country lane, she had become almost certain she would see it, and sure enough, it stood in the centre of the road, blocking the way forward.

Tasha leant forward from the back seat. "What are you doing, Sam?"

"Stating our business."

Ashley chuckled. "Leave the door open in case you have to leg it."

But Sam wasn't afraid. She approached the stag without any trepidation, for she understood that it had been intending to save her and her friends that day, exactly one year ago. It was a protector of the darkness that dwelt in the forest. A place called Frenzy.

The stag snorted as she approached, but it made no move to attack her.

Sam put out a hand to show she meant no danger. "I'm not here to cause any harm. Do you remember me?"

The stag obviously didn't reply, but the look in its deep brown eyes seemed to speak of recognition.

Sam carried on talking. "You tried to save us. You tried to save my friends, but we didn't listen. Thank you. I need to ask you to stand aside and let me visit again. I need to say goodbye to my friends. I need to know if they're okay."

The stag stared at her, and for a slight moment she thought it was going to charge her, but then it turned and trotted casually into the treeline.

Sam sighed. "Permission granted."

She got back in the car and drove the rest of the way, parking in the same spot AJ had one year ago. Echoes of her friend's voices – Greg, Ben, and AJ – echoed in her mind and caused her torment, but it didn't cause her to turn away. She and her remaining friends got out of the Land Rover and headed over the chain-link fence.

"You got what we need?" Sam asked Tasha.

Tasha nodded and shrugged off her pack. From inside she took a pair of bolt cutters. Their previous entrance had been repaired, but it took no time at all to make a new way in.

Ashley put a hand on Sam's shoulder. "You sure you want to do this?"

"Don't you?"

Ashley sighed and nodded. "Yeah, I do."

The three girls ducked through the gap in the fence and headed for the place that had haunted all of their nightmares for the last twelve months. They headed to Pagan's Grove. It was exactly the same, except for one key difference. Frenzy was gone. The great bronze helmet had been removed, along with the entire building. All that remained was a massive brick foundation and a collection of scraps.

After falling into the hole inside the ride, they had reached a lower chamber outside. The sun had been up and there were birds in the sky. They didn't need to escape the ride because whatever shelter had once housed the exit had fallen down. A pile of bricks was all that remained.

Sam had tried to climb back up the track, to get to AJ, but Tasha and Ashley had dragged her away. There was no hope that he would still be alive. That he had lasted as long as he had was testament to his courage and strength. He had fought long enough to see them safe, but Sam knew he would have dropped dead right after.

He had saved her, and right then at that moment she realised she had wasted her life by being just friends with a man she loved. It hurt her heart that they could have been so much more to each other. Instead, she had concentrated on a career she hated.

Now AJ was dead and the rest of her life made no sense.

The three girls had walked away from Saxon Hills like battlefield survivors. They leant on each other and limped along through the forest. Eventually they had made it to the main road and collapsed. A local builder had found them while driving past in his van and called an ambulance. At the hospital, Sam, Ashley, and Tasha had agreed not to tell the police anything until they had a story prepared.

The story went like this: they had gone to Saxon Hills to party, but it had turned into a nightmare when the boys had got drunk and injured themselves in the darkness of the ride. They kept it that simple, and refrained from further detail. It left the onus on the police to prove the real truth if they didn't believe it, and the real truth was something they would never discover.

Eventually the ride had been condemned as a death trap and knocked down. The police had performed their investigations, of course, but all they could find were three dead men inside a dangerous, derelict ride. The tragedy was enough as it was, without turning it into some greater mystery, so they closed the case and everyone moved on.

Except for Ashley, Tasha, and Sam. They had lost three men they loved.

"It's creepy being here again," said Tasha.

Sam nodded. She looked at the ruins of what had once been a terrifying place and couldn't believe what had taken place there. She still didn't really understand it, except that it had been beyond what most people understood about the world. There *was* more.

The sun was setting, which made it about the same time they had arrived before.

"It's time," said Sam.

Ashley smiled. She put down her pack and pulled out some beers. The plan was definitely not to get drunk and party. They were here for another reason. Tasha did the honours. She held up her beer and the others did the same. "To my brother. To Greg. And to AJ. We will always love you."

"Hear hear," said Ashley and Sam in tandem. Then they drank.

"You got one for me?" said a voice. The sound of it caused Tasha to freeze and drop her beer.

Out of the rubble, Ben appeared. Not the Ben they knew, because this Ben was walking. This Ben was smiling. Tasha looked like she might faint. Sam steadied her.

Tasha's bottom lip quivered. "B-B-Ben, you're alive?"

Ben shimmered in the dusky sunlight. "Nah, sis, but I'm here anyway. I missed you."

"Y-Y-You're here? Really here?"

Ben smirked. "Yeah, sis. We all are."

AJ and Greg stepped forward from the rubble. "We waited," said AJ. "As long as we could."

"We knew you'd miss us," said Greg with a warm smile on his face that he had rarely worn in life. "Thought we'd throw you a bone. You're looking fine, Ash. I hope you're happy."

Sam was transfixed on AJ. He was even more beautiful than he had been in life. His hair had gone from blonde to golden, and his skin seemed to shine like fine diamonds. "A-Are you okay, AJ?"

He took her hands in his and smiled. "I am now."

He leant forward and kissed her, a perfect moment that seemed to go on forever and yet lasted no time at all. Then he was gone. They were all gone. The three girls stood alone.

"Did that just happen?" asked Ashley.

Sam sipped her beer. "It doesn't matter. All that matters is that we got to say goodbye."

They poured a beer on the ground for the men they had loved.

WANT FREE BOOKS?

Don't miss out on your FREE Iain Rob Wright horror starter pack. Five free bestselling horror novels sent straight to your inbox. No strings attached.

CLICK HERE TO GET YOUR 5 FREE BOOKS

PLEA FROM THE AUTHOR

Hey, Reader. So you got to the end of my book. I hope that means you enjoyed it. Whether or not you did, I would just like to thank you for giving me your valuable time to try and entertain you. I am truly blessed to have such a fulfilling job, but I only have that job because of people like you; people kind enough to give my books a chance and spend their hard-earned money buying them. For that I am eternally grateful.

If you would like to find out more about my other books then please visit my website for full details. You can find it at:

www.iainrobwright.com.

Also feel free to contact me on Facebook, Twitter, or email (all details on the website), as I would love to hear from you.

If you enjoyed this book and would like to help, then you could think about leaving a review on Amazon, Goodreads, or anywhere else that readers visit. The most important part of how well a book sells is how many positive reviews it has, so if you leave me one then you are directly helping me to continue on this journey as a fulltime writer. Thanks in advance to anyone who does. It means a lot.

Iain Rob Wright is one of the UK's most successful horror and suspense writers, with novels including the critically acclaimed, THE FINAL WINTER; the disturbing bestseller, ASBO; and the wicked screamfest, THE HOUSEMATES.

His work is currently being adapted for graphic novels, audio books, and foreign audiences. He is an active member of the Horror Writer Association and a massive animal lover.

www.iainrobwright.com
FEAR ON EVERY PAGE

For more information
www.iainrobwright.com
iain.robert.wright@hotmail.co.uk

Copyright © 2019 by Iain Rob Wright

Cover Photographs © Shutterstock

Artwork by Stuart Bache at Books Covers Ltd

Editing by Richard Sheehan

All rights reserved.

No part of this book may be reproduced in any form or by any electronic or mechanical means, including information storage and retrieval systems, without written permission from the author, except for the use of brief quotations in a book review.

❦ Created with Vellum

Printed in Great Britain
by Amazon